DISNEP
M⊚ANA 2

rhcbooks.com

ISBN 978-0-7364-4506-1 (trade)

Printed in the United States of America

10 9 8 7 6 5 4 3 2 1

DISNEY
M⊚ANA 2

THE JUNIOR NOVELIZATION

Adapted by Elizabeth Rudnick

Random House 🏠 New York

Deep in the jungle, far from the shores of Motunui, everything was still. The sun's early-morning rays peeked through the tree canopy, illuminating pieces of the vine-covered jungle floor. Occasional bird-song provided the only sound besides the ocean waves gently crashing against the shore.

Until . . .

WHOOSH!

Moana, master wayfinder, raced through the jungle, her brow furrowed in concentration and her breath coming in gasps. Carrying her oar, Moana was running from something that was grunting loudly.

She shouted and skidded to a halt, catching herself just before plummeting into a deep ravine. The mountain loomed. She turned and looked behind her. The beast was gaining on her. There was only one thing to do.

Moana jumped. For one long breath, she was suspended over the ravine. Then, with a thud, she landed on the rocky outcropping on the other side. Steadying herself with her oar, she took a moment to catch her breath.

The grunts of the beast grew louder as it came closer. And closer . . .

"Pua!" Moana smiled across the ravine as her loyal, adorable friend appeared. The pig was gasping for air, his little legs shaking from the effort of the chase. He met Moana's gaze. Even from a distance, it was easy to see that he'd had enough.

"Almost there! Just an easy little hop," she called out in encouragement. Her gaze drifted down. "Kinda."

Pua looked down. Way down. Thick, sharp brambles covered the rocky floor of the ravine. He lifted his head and gave Moana another look. She knew exactly what that look meant. Pua wasn't going a step farther on his own.

✱ ✱ ✱

Moana's fingers ached and her legs cramped as she climbed up the side of the mountain. On her back, Pua dangled in a sling she had made, making little fearful grunts. Moana didn't exactly blame him. Under her hands and feet was nothing but a sheer wall of rock— rock that kept breaking apart at random intervals.

"Hey, you wanted to come this time," Moana said as she swung her arm up and over the rock ledge. Her fingers found flat ground and she let out a triumphant shout. They had made it to the top! Pulling herself and Pua up and over, she came face to face with . . .

"Heihei?" Moana said, staring at the bug-eyed rooster. "How?"

Heihei stared back at her blankly. Shaking her head, Moana stood up. They were atop the highest peak of a small, deserted island. Cerulean sea surrounded them, glistening in the morning light. For one long moment, Moana allowed herself to enjoy the feeling of discovery. It never got old, the sensation of standing in a new place.

Reaching for her necklace, she pulled out a small shell and placed it on the ground, like she had done many times before on many other empty islands. Then she took the conch shell from her belt, lifted it to her lips, and blew.

The sound rang out over the ocean waves, clear to the horizon. Moana strained to listen, hoping.

"Hear anything?" she asked her friends. Glancing back, she saw that Pua's ears were lifted, his expression serious as he listened, too.

Sighing, Moana turned back to the sea. "There's gotta be others out here. Other villages, people," she said with determination. "And one day, someone's gonna . . ." Her voice trailed off. In the distance she heard what sounded like an answering conch. Her eyes grew wide as hope filled her heart.

Then she looked over and realized that the sound was coming from Heihei, who was choking on a shell. He was standing on one end of a long, log-like rock. At the other end sat Pua, watching Heihei with amusement as the rooster spit up the shell.

"Never change," Moana said, smiling despite her disappointment. In answer, Heihei continued to stare blankly at her. Then the rock he and Pua were standing on began to shift. They were about to fall off the cliff!

"Wait! Whoa! No, no, no!" Moana shouted. She lunged for Pua and Heihei. Moana had only a moment to realize what was about to happen before she and her friends went tumbling over the edge, disappearing into the jungle below.

They landed with a loud thud in the dirt. Moana took a moment to look around. Her warm brown eyes widened. Nestled in the overgrown vines and shadowed by the heavy overgrowth of leaves was a small altar. A *human*-made altar.

CLUCK!

Heihei's head popped up from behind the altar, making Moana jump. She started to laugh at the silly rooster, and then she noticed something stuck to his head. She squinted. It looked like a small piece of pottery.

Moving closer, Moana gently pulled the item off Heihei. She held it in her hands, her heart racing with excitement.

Rubbing off the thin layer of dirt that covered the surface of the pottery relic, she felt something underneath her fingers. It was carving or writing of some kind. She brought the object into a patch of sunlight and looked closer. There was an island carved into the pottery, with a constellation of stars etched above and people on the ground.

With her excitement growing, Moana let out a happy shout. She finally had proof that there were other people out there!

She had to return home and show her village what she had found. Maybe her father would know what the constellation meant and which island was pictured on the pottery.

"Heihei! You dumb, beautiful chicken!" she cheered.

Laughing, she turned and raced off toward the shore. A beat later, she stopped and looked back at Pua and Heihei. The pair were still standing by the altar, looking confused. Or, rather, Pua looked confused. Heihei looked like he always did.

"What are you waiting for?" she said, beckoning them to follow. "Let's go home!"

CHAPTER 2

Moana inhaled deeply. She could feel Motunui's pull like a gentle hand tugging her home. She loved exploring where there was always something on the horizon, a promise of new discovery.

But she also loved coming home.

Things were always the same, yet different. Children sat beneath the thatched roof of the storytelling fale, listening to Moni, the village historian. He told stories of their ancestors, the original voyagers, as well as the newest tale—the one of Moana and Maui, demigod of the Wind and Sea, and their journey to restore the heart of Te Fiti. Farmers worked in the fields, tending to harvests that would feed the village.

Now whenever Moana scanned the ocean beyond the reef, she could see voyagers from her village riding the waves in canoes of their own.

Lifting her eyes, she saw the familiar reef appear, and beyond that, her village. A smile broke across her face when she spotted her father, Chief Tui, racing toward her on his canoe. For a man who had once forbidden her from going past the reef, he now spent quite a lot of time beyond it himself. A moment later, his canoe crested a wave and splashed down near hers.

"Race 'the chief' to shore?" he asked with a smile.

"Aw, Dad," Moana replied, teasing. "It's never much of a race."

Before he could argue, she was off, steering her canoe over the breakers and toward home. Behind her she heard her father's laughter as the air whipped her thick brown hair around her face.

Moments later, her canoe raced up onto the sand. Moana didn't even wait for it to come to a complete stop before she jumped off. As the villagers came down to greet her, she began to unload her canoe, revealing the treasures she had collected on her most recent journey: A heavy basket of strangely shaped fruit. An enormous clam.

"Coming through, coming through!" Moana's friend Loto shouted with her axe-like tool, called an adze, in hand. She pushed past the other villagers and skidded to a halt. Loto was always moving, always inventing, always thinking. When Moana had returned to the village three years before, it had changed everything. People wanted boats and new ways to fish. Loto was happy to use her smarts to help. Now the girl's eyes ping-ponged between Moana and the canoe.

"New canoe. How'd she hold up?" Loto asked. "Lay it on me."

Moana paused. She knew that Loto would take to heart whatever she said. And try to fix it. Immediately. She eyed Loto's adze. "I mean," she began, "it takes a bit to rotate the sail, but—"

"Got it!" Loto didn't let her finish. Before Moana could stop her, Loto had jumped onto the canoe and cut down the mast with her adze.

Moana bit back a laugh. At least she knew that Loto would build her something better. Glancing around to make sure no one had been hit by the suddenly falling mast, Moana saw her father pulling his own boat to shore. Hopping off, he made his way over.

"So, how'd it go this time?" he asked.

Something between pride and relief filled Moana. She had been searching for so long, and now . . . She pulled out the piece of pottery and handed it to her father. As he examined it, she filled him in on what had happened. "There was a stack of stones, by a mountain—well, I fell off the mountain—but then . . . This isn't from our village. I don't even know what it's made of, but it's proof." She stopped and caught her breath. Then she nodded at the carvings. "Dad, there are other people out there. And now we know where. And that island"—she pointed to the island depicted on the pottery—"I think that's where I'm gonna find them. I just have to figure out how to find those stars."

Chief Tui smiled. He thought maybe Moana should get some rest. He loved her enthusiasm, but she seemed overexcited, and she was still his daughter. He wanted to take care of her. Before he could suggest it, a loud shriek pierced the air.

"MOANA!"

A moment later, a young girl burst onto the beach, bulldozing her way through the gathered villagers.

Moana's face broke into a huge grin. "Little sis!" she said, pulling the girl up into her arms and tightly squeezing her.

"BIG SIS!" three-year-old Simea said back, her smile mirroring Moana's. Then she frowned and pouted her little lips. She grabbed Moana's face and gave her a staredown. "You were gone forever."

Moana held back a laugh. Simea could be dramatic. Yet coming home to her was one of the things Moana loved most. "It was three days, but I missed you every—"

Simea didn't let her finish. "What did you bring me?"

"Bring you?" Moana repeated.

"You said you'd bring me a present."

Moana tapped her chin, as if trying to remember. "Huh . . . Well, let me see. . . ." Then, with a triumphant smile, she lifted up the piece of pottery she had found and showed her sister.

Simea was not impressed. "What's it do?" she asked.

Moana didn't answer. It would be pointless to try to explain to Simea what the object meant. She was only three years old, after all.

Moana needed to show her.

Entering the cavern of the ancestors, Moana felt the same rush of excitement she had the first time she ever saw the huge space filled with ancient canoes. Then she had been an untried wayfinder who'd felt the ocean's call but hadn't answered it. Now? Now she was a skilled voyager who had befriended a demigod. Even so, this place would never stop making her heart soar.

Beside her, she felt her little sister's excitement bubbling over. Simea was bouncing on her toes. Her hands covered her eyes, but she couldn't wait a second longer. Simea peeked through her fingers.

Her little jaw dropped as she took in the cavern for the first time. "Whoa," Simea whispered.

"This is a place of our ancestors, where I learned our people were voyagers. . . ." Moana smiled, watching her sister take it all in. A few years ago, she had worn the same expression herself. "Where Gramma showed me who we are." Her voice hitched slightly at the mention of her grandmother. She still missed her.

Simea's eyes lit up. She knew this story. "Gramma, she said you grab Maui by the ear and tell him, 'I am Moana of Motunui, you will board my boat and restore the heart of Te Fiti.'"

Simea's serious expression was so adorable that Moana had to hold back a smile. "Pretty good," Moana admitted.

"Yeah," Simea said smugly as she plopped down on the canoe and stared over at the far cavern wall. An image of Te Fiti was carved into the stone. "How long did it take?" she asked.

"Few weeks," Moana answered, sitting down beside her.

"*Weeks?*" Simea repeated dramatically. "That's longer than forever!"

Moana chuckled. "I know. But it was important. *And* if I hadn't gone, I never would've become a wayfinder. Like our ancient chiefs." She pointed her finger toward more images carved into the walls, depicting more of Motunui's history.

Her eyes moved wistfully over the carvings, landing on one depicting the last great navigator, Tautai Vasa. Despite its age, the carving still seemed to gleam, as if lit from inside with the energy of the skilled voyager. Holding Simea's hand, Moana walked along, viewing the other images, other stories told through the art. There were Te Kā and Te Fiti. Great and fearsome monsters roaming the ocean. Like the siapos that hung in Moni's storytelling fale.

These images and the stories Moana's grandmother had once told had helped inspire her original journey.

And she felt in her bones that they were pushing her toward a new one now. Beside her, Simea stared up at the images, awe on her little face.

"Before Maui stole Te Fiti's heart . . . and darkness spread"—Moana couldn't help lowering her voice, adopting the tone Gramma Tala used to take when she told the story of their ancestors—"Tautai Vasa wanted to connect our island to all the people of the entire ocean."

Simea's eyes went wide.

"And as a wayfinder, it's my job to finish what he started." Moana held up the piece of pottery she had brought back from her latest voyage. "And *this* is my first clue how." Her voice drifted off, the immense weight of what she had said heavy on her shoulders. It would mean everything to her to be the voyager Tautai Vasa had once been.

Simea waited a beat and then scrunched up her nose, breaking the seriousness of the moment. "You should make Maui do it, so you can stay with *me*!"

"Well, if he ever shows up and you finally get to meet him, *you* grab him by the ear and tell him that." Her eyes darted to the image of Maui carved into the wall. She hadn't seen him since her return to Motunui,

and she missed him. Not that she would admit it out loud.

Besides, he was probably very busy doing important demigod stuff.

Wherever he was.

Far from Motunui, deep under the sea, the world was silent. The sun's rays filtered weakly through the water, casting shadows on the shoals and formations of rocks and sand. A group of smelt swam in sync through the water, creating patterns. As they passed through a beam of light, their silver scales flashed momentarily. It was peaceful beneath the waves. Sound was muted, the distant noises of the shore far above unable to penetrate the salty water.

Suddenly, an unexpected movement startled the school of smelt. They scattered, their choreographed formation breaking apart. A moment later, an enormous blue whale swam by, its large body gracefully maneuvering through the water. If the fish had had more time to observe the huge creature, they would have noticed that this was no ordinary blue whale. On its side was a series of tattoos that swirled and spread.

The whale increased its speed as it headed toward some craggy coral. Just before it hit the rough coral wall, it shot upward, racing toward the surface. A moment later, it burst into the air. Up, up, up the enormous creature rose. The sun sparkled off the drops of water that fell from the whale as it hovered before dropping back down. But the whale never hit the water. Instead, it transformed into a giant hawk.

It was Maui!

The shape-shifting demigod let out a loud caw as he rocketed just above the ocean's surface. A trail of white water was left in his wake. The demigod didn't register the spray from below or the expanding clouds above. His hawk-like gaze was fixed on the fog bank straight ahead. Dense and impossibly thick, it seemed to grow with each passing moment. But Maui didn't slow. Instead, with another flap of his giant wings, he flew right into the fog bank and was instantly swallowed by the mist.

"Chee Hoo!" he cried.

There was a moment of silence, and then a single *BOOM* echoed over the waves. It was as if an enormous door had just been slammed shut. Shock waves rippled out from the fog.

And then the water stilled. The fog faded, leaving nothing but water for as far as the eye could see.

With his hook in hand, Maui stood inside the fog, watching as it swirled and shifted around him unnaturally, as if manipulated by some invisible hand—which was a possibility, Maui reasoned, since he was far beyond the realm of humans. Holding up his glowing hook like a lantern, he stepped forward. In front of him, the fog began to settle around what appeared to be a huge, pearl-like orb.

Maui's eyes narrowed as the light from the pearl illuminated the tattoos that covered his body. Each told a story from Maui's past. They were moments of heroism inked permanently on his skin as a reminder to all who met him who he was—and how much he had done for humans. Humans were, in fact, why he was here now, in this unknown realm of the gods

looking at the pinkish-white ball in front of him. At least, he *thought* that might be why he was here. These missions to benefit humans didn't always come with clear instructions.

He thought about what he and Moana had been through. Racing over the waves, bringing the heart of Te Fiti back, facing Te Kā. He hadn't seen any of that coming. But had it been worth it? Totally. Plus it didn't hurt that he'd gotten his hook back at the end of it all.

Suddenly, from somewhere behind him, Maui heard flapping wings, the noise echoing through the fog. He shivered. The sound grew louder. It was everywhere and nowhere at once.

A bat flew past him, reminding him of where he was and the danger that could be lurking. He turned away from the pearl, slowly spinning in a circle, scanning the fog for any signs of a threat.

He straightened his shoulders, took a deep breath, and shouted . . . "Yoo-hoo?" The greeting came out a little higher-pitched than he had intended.

On his chest, Mini Maui, a tattoo that was a small image of himself, sprang to life. Mini Maui hit his own forehead as if to say, "*That's* your big greeting?"

Clearing his throat, Maui continued to address

whatever was hiding in the fog. "I'm not here to cause trouble," he announced in a deeper voice. He nodded. That was better. "Just a super-chiseled demigod passing through. Lot's changed since I've been gone, including me." It was an understatement. Maui had been transformed. Not in the literal sense—he did that all the time. But meeting Moana had made him a better person—or, rather, a better demigod—which was why he now found himself in this realm of the gods that he'd sworn he would never return to, trying to get the attention of a demigoddess he'd hoped never to see again.

From somewhere in the fog came the sound of a woman's laughter. It echoed eerily throughout the chamber as if it came from every direction. Maui's head whipped around, trying to pinpoint the sound, but all he could see was a flash of a silhouette here, then there.

"*Evolved*, have we?" the female voice said. "Just like that?"

Maui frowned. He recognized that voice. It was Matangi, the purple-eyed powerful demigoddess he unfortunately needed to face.

"Well, a thousand years on Fish-Stink Island will get anyone to question their choices." As he spoke, he swung his glowing hook around, hoping to reveal

the demigoddess attached to the voice. "Now I'm all about doing the right thing. Ha!" Spotting movement, he lunged forward, swinging his hook. But it was just bats. They swirled around him, surrounding him like a tornado. Anger flared in him. He was growing tired of Matangi's tricks. He swung his hook faster and harder. The bats dispersed quickly, except one that had the unfortunate luck of being struck by the hook. The creature was jettisoned into the darkness, its squeak fading as it disappeared from sight.

"Enough games. My beef is with your boss, not his . . . weird gatekeeper. Which, to be clear, is you. Open the path and I'll be on my way," Maui said.

From inside the mist, Matangi let out a long sigh. "Demigods," she drawled, her eye roll evident in her tone. "Finally free and all you wanna do is pick another fight."

Maui's thick eyebrows drew together. "Nalo started it."

"And you'll finish it?" Matangi sneered. "Team up with the precious little human again?"

Maui clenched his fists but kept his face neutral. He needed to hide the fact that he considered Moana a friend. He had to protect her from the danger Matangi posed. "Team?" he repeated with a laugh. "The girl

with the canoe and the goofy chicken? We weren't a team. I just used her to get my hook."

On his chest, Mini Maui flicked him, his message clear: *That's not true at all.* Maui subtly shook his head and shot him his own silent message: *Don't worry, I got this.* Mini Maui wasn't convinced.

And neither was Matangi. She scoffed. The fog shifted and swirled, revealing the floor upon which Maui stood. It was covered by a massive petroglyph showing a shadowy god looming over the island of Motufetū. "Nalo is a *god,* Maui. Follow this path and he will destroy you. And then he'll destroy her, too."

Maui's expression darkened. "This is between him and me," he hissed. "Moana has nothing to do with it."

It was true. He hadn't seen her since they had restored the heart of Te Fiti. Sure, he had hoped to surprise her. But things were obviously not going his way.

There was a beat as Maui's words echoed off the chamber. And then . . . chaos! Hundreds of bat wings flapped in the air, the sound deafening. Glowing purple eyes appeared through the fog. A moment later, Matangi materialized. She moved toward Maui, her purple eyes boring into him. He gulped as she approached. Matangi had always been a bit . . . well, creepy. And time had made her only more so.

A corner of her smile lifted cruelly as she reached out and ran a long fingernail over Maui's chest, her sharp talon lingering over his most recent tattoo—the one of Moana. As she looked at the black lines, she shook her head. "You made her a wayfinder, Maui. So now she has *everything* to do with it."

Maui felt anger flood his body. He tightened his grip on his hook, which had started to glow again. His nostrils flared. He refused to let Moana be hurt or threatened. And it was clear that Matangi and the god she protected were not going to let him do things peacefully.

Fine, then. He would fight. Launching himself into the air, he pulled his hook back. At the same time, Matangi exploded into a hundred bats.

The battle was on.

The stars were just starting to twinkle in the sky as the village of Motunui came to life. Fires blazed, their red-orange flames casting a warm glow on those who were gathered. A group of dancers swayed their skirts to the beat of the drums while children chased one another between the fales.

Moana's mind raced as she made her way through the village. Her thoughts bounced back and forth between Maui, Tautai Vasa, the sea, her sister, and the pottery relic.

Her mother, Sina, walked beside her, eyes on the

relic in Moana's hands. She gave her daughter a hug, so proud.

As Sina made her way over to her other daughter, Simea, one of the villagers approached Moana with a haku lei in her hands. She gestured for Moana to lean forward, then placed the collection of flowers on top of her head. The villager turned and disappeared into the rapidly growing throng around Moana.

Loto appeared, her ever-present adze in hand, startling Moana. "I'd like a sample of that," Loto said, reaching toward the pottery relic.

Jokingly—sort of—Moana pulled the relic closer to herself. She loved Loto, but there was no way she was letting the relic get anywhere near that adze. She needed the recovered object to stay in one piece at least until she figured out the answers to her questions.

Even Moni, who prided himself in knowing everything about everything, seemed perplexed when he, too, appeared by her side to stare at the object. His eyes narrowed, and Moana knew the wheels in his brain were whirling.

Moana continued to move toward the center of the village. Everyone was in a festive mood. And yet, glancing at the feast that had been laid out, she realized that no one was eating. Why was no one eating?

Clearing her throat, she yelled, "Well, eat up! Don't want the pork getting cold!" A groan at her feet made Moana look down. *Oops,* she thought, spotting Pua. *Gotta stop doing that.*

Just then, the music went quiet. It felt as though the village collectively held its breath as Chief Tui approached. One by one, torches were lit.

"Moana, my dear, tonight isn't just a feast," Chief Tui said as Sina and Simea joined him.

Stepping forward, he put a strong arm around Moana's shoulder and squeezed. Her heart began to pound.

Chief Tui led his daughter forward, allowing the villagers to form a circle around them. "Long ago, there was a title given to the last great wayfinder with dreams as big as yours. More than a chief: a tautai. Leader of land and sea." He paused, taking in the significance of this moment. "My dear, would you honor us tonight by accepting this title—our people's first tautai in a thousand years?"

Moana's breath hitched. Was this really happening?

"And show us all just how far we'll go," he finished, proud tears in his eyes.

The words flooded through her, the importance of this request hitting her hard. Tautai? Like Tautai Vasa?

Was she really worthy of such a title? Her eyes drifted from her father to her mother, and then her sister, who was looking up at her with total admiration. And in that moment, she knew the answer.

Smiling, Moana nodded. Yes. It was a definite yes.

A short while later, Moana found herself sitting across from her father in the fale closest to the water's edge. It felt fitting for the official ceremony naming her tautai to occur near the water that was so much a part of her. Moana looked at her people happily. She felt their immense love, as well as the responsibility of what had been asked of her.

Outside, the ocean waves gently broke against the beach in a soothing rhythm. A breeze picked up, rippling over the crowd, marking a change in the weather. But no one besides Sina seemed to notice. They were focused on Moana and her father.

Chief Tui began. "Tonight we drink from our ancestors' bowl, as Tautai Vasa once did, to bestow this title on you. To connect to our past, our present, and the future that lies beyond." Lifting a bowl in his hand, he tilted it, letting some of the liquid inside splash onto the dirt floor as an offering to the ancestors. Then he drank the rest. "May the ancestors continue to guide us."

Then he looked at Moana. It was her turn. Stepping forward, Moni offered her a cup of her own. Moana held it in steady hands as she gazed around at those she loved. Then she raised the cup and echoed her father's words. "May the ancestors continue to guide us."

But as she raised the cup to her lips, she saw her reflection in the liquid and paused. Something was there, rippling on the surface. A shiver ran through her. Something strange was happening. Outside the fale, the wind grew stronger, whipping through the leaves. Suddenly, a crackling noise seemed to come from all sides of the fale. An eerie light began to build around them, making the space glow brighter and brighter until . . .

CRACK!

A bolt of lightning flashed in the air.

Then everything went black.

Moana's eyes snapped open. Above her, a ring of clouds created a halo around a clear, star-filled sky. In the middle, brighter than the rest, a constellation brilliantly twinkled.

Suddenly, the ground beneath her feet shifted. Moana stumbled, trying to keep her balance. Looking down, she realized that she was no longer in the fale. Instead, she was standing on the deck of a massive, ancient canoe. When she looked up, she gasped. The same images etched on the relic she'd discovered were stitched into the sail: the same island, the same constellation.

As her gaze traveled farther along the canoe, she spotted a lone man standing at the bow. The wayfinder cut an imposing figure as he stared out across the sea.

Moana knew exactly who this was. "Tautai Vasa," she whispered in awe.

Somehow she knew that while she could see him, the legendary wayfinder—and the others operating the large boat—were unaware of her presence. She was witnessing a moment from the past. But how? Why?

She followed Tautai Vasa's gaze. Her eyes grew wider still. He was looking up at the bright constellation! It matched the one on the relic exactly.

"Motufetū," he said to himself, his expression worried. "Should be under the stars. . . ."

As Moana watched his eyes move from the stars to the waters around them, she realized why Tautai Vasa seemed so worried. A huge storm had encircled them. Darkness had descended upon the sea, turning the blue waters black. The wind picked up and ripped at the sail. The world was thrust into inky chaos.

"Bind the sail! Light the oar!" Tautai Vasa called out to his crew.

"Vasa? We're lost!" shouted one of the voyagers.

Tautai Vasa stood, shaking his head, terror evident on his face. He didn't have the answers for what to do next. The unpredictable, dangerous storm was growing wilder by the moment. The same feeling washed over Moana, as though she was experiencing every emotion Tautai Vasa was in the moment. She struggled to stay upright in the strong wind.

With a lurch, Tautai Vasa's crew was thrown off the canoe. He lunged to save them, but he wasn't fast enough. Tautai Vasa landed hard on the deck. He turned and looked up. Something above terrified him.

Then the canoe was slammed by a massive dark wave. Moana was thrown backward into the water.

She sank beneath the surface, the loud sounds of the storm instantly muted by the water. But she wasn't sinking. The water was unlike anything she had ever encountered before. She seemed to hover in the thick substance, suspended. She watched as an enormous whale shark slowly swam past. Its sides were covered with glowing tattoos.

Awed by the creature's majestic beauty, she reached a hand through the water . . .

. . . only to suddenly find herself back on the shores of Motunui.

The beach was empty. The island seemed deserted. Moana looked around, confused. What was happening? "Where are my people?" Moana whispered to herself.

"Tautai Moana."

Spinning at the sound of her name, she found herself once again looking at Tautai Vasa. Only this time, he was aware of her presence. His body glowed and shimmered in the darkness. Moana could sense that he was troubled.

"You've come so far, but you must go farther. You must reconnect our people, or this is how our story ends," he said mysteriously. "In isolation there is no future. Find the island of Motufetū, reconnect our people, restore the never-ending chain . . ."

His voice was fading. Panic flooded Moana. He couldn't go yet. She didn't know what he meant. "Where? It's under stars I've never seen," she said.

"The fire in the sky will guide you," Tautai Vasa explained.

"Wait, I don't even know how far it is," Moana said, her voice small and full of uncertainty.

"Farther than I was able to go," he replied cryptically. "Find Motufetū, reconnect us all."

And then he was gone. In the water he returned to his whale shark form. As he swam off, he left a trail in his wake, like a comet in the sea. It led straight to an island that appeared to hover over the water a short distance from Motunui.

When the whale shark reached the island, glowing channels surrounded the island, lighting up the sea and Motunui.

As she watched, the island and the water began to glow brighter and brighter.

Could this be Motufetū?

Moana felt certain of it.

CHAPTER 5

Moana jolted awake. The beach was gone. Tautai Vasa, the glowing island, the comet-like trail—all gone. She was back in the fale. Her mother sat by her side, worry etched on her face.

"Shh, you're okay," she said to Moana in a soothing voice.

"What . . . what happened?" Moana asked, trying to focus. Her whole body ached. She felt like she had been dragged over a coral reef.

"Well, you kinda got struck by lightning," her mother replied.

It came back to Moana in a flash as bright as the lightning that had hit her. The ceremony. The gathered village. The strange storm. She picked up the pottery relic.

Sina's eyes filled with surprise and concern.

"Mom, I saw this island," she said softly, holding up the relic. "I need to find Moni." If anyone could help her find out more about the mysterious island, it was him.

Moana and Sina entered the storytelling fale where Moni and Chief Tui were examining a very old siapo that Moni held in his hands. The images on the fabric were faded with age and hard to see. When he saw them enter, his eyes bounced between Moana, her mom, and the siapo. He had a bit of a wild look about him, like he had spent too much time staring at siapos.

"I found this. It's an old story," Moni began, excited as always to explain their peoples' history.

Moana took a closer look at the siapo, and her eyes grew wide. It was the island from her vision. Motufetū.

Moana listened closely, determined not to miss

anything. Like Gramma Tala, Moni had a way of telling stories that brought them to life.

Moni continued. "Motufetū. Where the channels of the ocean came together, connecting the people of the sea. Until it was lost."

"Lost?" asked Moana.

Moni held up another siapo. Moana could see this image more clearly. A raging god rose above, cursing the island.

"Hidden in a terrible storm, a curse of a jealous god who wanted to separate humans. To make us weaker." Moni pointed to the image of the god cursing Motufetū.

Moana recalled Tautai Vasa's words and echoed them. "In isolation, our story ends."

"Unless someone can find Motufetū and step on its shores again," Moni explained to Moana.

"That's how you break the curse?" asked Moana.

"Yeah," Moni replied. With his story finished, Moni fell silent, as did the rest of the fale. The weight of what Moni had just said was not lost on any of those gathered. To find a hidden island? Brave a terrible storm and step on its shores? The danger and responsibility of such a quest were nearly impossible to comprehend.

Slowly, Sina turned to look at Moana. Her eyes were

filled with fear. "And the ancestors have called you to do it," she said softly.

Moni's eyes revealed that he understood the incredible burden Moana had just been given.

Moana gulped. She was the tautai, after all—but she didn't exactly know where to find this cursed island. All she had was Tautai Vasa's cryptic message, Moni's story, and the pottery relic she had found. But she had to try.

Her thoughts were interrupted by the sound of someone crying. Moana's head whipped around. Simea was peeking out from behind one of the fale's pillars, tears on her cheeks. She had heard everything.

"I don't want you to be tautai," she said, sniffling. "I don't want you to leave anymore."

Moana's mouth opened and shut. She didn't know what to say to her little sister. Of course she didn't want to leave her family. "Simea, I—"

Suddenly, a brilliant light outside began to glow, illuminating the fale and saving Moana from having to finish her reply.

"CHIEF!" a villager cried.

What, Moana wondered, *is happening now?*

With the others close on her heels, Moana raced out of the fale. It appeared that night had turned to day. The whole village was illuminated in a red-orange glow. Following the gaze of the villagers already outside, Moana gasped.

There in the sky above them was a huge comet. It was like the one she had seen Tautai Vasa leave in his wake. His words came back to her: *The fire in the sky will guide you.* This had to be what he had been talking about.

"A fire in the sky," she said quietly. "He wants me to follow it."

Worry flashed over Chief Tui's face as he looked down at Moana. The meaning of what she said hit him. "We don't even know where that island is. This could take forever . . . a lifetime," he said, his voice heavy with emotion.

Moana's breath hitched. Tautai Vasa didn't come back at all.

"We need to meet with the council," Chief Tui said. "It's too big a—"

Moni cut him off. "Chief, she has to leave, like, now." He glanced at Moana. "It won't wait."

Under the red-orange sky, the villagers turned to Moana. She felt their gazes on her, the burden heavy.

She looked back up at the sky. Moni was right. The comet wouldn't stay for long.

"You can't leave," Simea said.

Chief Tui tried to reassure his youngest daughter, but it was pointless.

Simea shook her head. *"You can't leave!"* This time her voice was a desperate shout, the words echoing across the beach.

"Simea—" Moana started.

But the little girl didn't wait. Turning, she raced off, her shoulders shaking with her sobs. Sina hesitated for one beat, her eyes lingering on Moana, before she also turned, following Simea.

Moana watched them go, her eyes welling with tears. Emotions battled inside her. Sadness. Fear. Anger . . . excitement. Beside her, her father stood silently, waiting for her to speak.

"I know what I have to do," she said. "But *forever*? To give up my island? My people? My family? How can I? How can the ancestors ask so much of me?"

"Who else would they ask?" Chief Tui replied. A sad smile tugged at his mouth. But then he nodded, resolved. With one more smile and a squeeze of her shoulder, he went to Sina and Simea.

Alone, Moana made her way to the shore and sat.

She had to leave. Of this she was certain. But the possibility of never seeing her family or village again crushed her. They were woven into the very fabric of her being. If she were to go so far from home, would she still be herself? Motunui was in her blood the same way the sea was. But if she could never again step on its shores, who would she become?

She knew her family and the entire village would always be by her side even if she was far from home. She wanted to be brave and make her ancestors and people proud. She felt the call of the comet's light, just as she had felt the call of the ocean years before. But this voyage felt different from her last. She felt a surge of fear at the thought of the task ahead. The thought of being gone from her home forever was nearly unbearable.

Suddenly, the water in front of her began to glow blue. The light grew brighter as a manta ray with glowing tattoos appeared in the lagoon.

"Gramma!" Moana cried as the familiar spirit of her grandmother appeared on the shore. Gramma Tala opened her arms wide. Moana didn't hesitate. She raced to her, sinking into her loving embrace. Gramma Tala ran her hand over Moana's hair.

Together the pair made their way to the rocks that lined the lagoon. They began to sway to a silent song.

As they did, Moana's heart ached. She had done this very thing so many times with Gramma Tala. It was a part of who she was, just like this island. The island she was going to have to leave soon.

Moana's movements were off, out of sync with her grandmother's. Gramma Tala kept swaying. "Oh, what are you so worried about?" she asked. Her voice was gentle, her eyes warm.

Moana sighed. "I know I need to go. It's just . . ." She hesitated, searching for the words. ". . . not what I expected."

Gramma Tala nodded. "I died and now I'm a manta ray," she replied. "When I was your age, you think I thought that would be my story?" She smiled, softly nudging Moana's hip with her own.

"Simea will never understand. How could I?" she whispered.

"You didn't want to leave me, either," Gramma Tala pointed out. "But here we are. Together still, just a little different."

"My island is a part of me. If I couldn't come home . . ." Moana's voice trailed off. Just saying the words aloud made her feel sick.

Gramma Tala stopped moving and gently placed her hands on Moana's arms. "Moana, I can't see where your story leads," she said, her voice soothing. "But we never stop choosing who we are." She moved from the rocks, walking into the shallows of the water. "The fire in the sky won't wait forever."

And then Gramma Tala transformed back into a glowing manta ray that darted around the lagoon. Soon the manta ray swam away. As the distance between Moana and her grew, the comet in the sky became brighter.

Moana knew her grandmother was right. The comet wouldn't be in the sky forever. She had to leave as soon as possible.

"I am Moana of Motunui. I will sail to a new sky, break the curse, and then . . . I *will* return home," she promised herself.

CHAPTER
6

"**M**oana, you need a crew," her mother said as they looked over Moana's canoe. "And Heihei and Pua don't count." She gestured to where the rooster and the pig stood. Heihei looked oblivious, as usual. Pua looked offended.

Her mother wasn't wrong. But to ask people to come with her? "It's the *other* side of the ocean. How could I ask them to—"

Sina stopped her. "Our people will rise if you let them."

42

Moana considered her mother's words. She was right. "Well, then I'm gonna need a bigger canoe," she said. She knew exactly who could help her with that.

Moana found Loto in her boathouse. She was bouncing all over the small space, a whirl of motion. As soon as Moana told her what she needed, Loto began to put together a model. "Yes! Brand-new—" she said, holding up a model canoe. "Sleek, double-hulled design. My best canoe yet. Top-of-the-line upgrades. Your crew's gonna love—"

"Loto!" Moana jumped in, stopping Loto mid-sentence. When her mother had told her she needed a crew—a human crew—she hadn't been sure who she would bring. But suddenly, she knew at least one person who needed to join. "I'd like you *on* the crew."

"Oh . . ." Loto paused for just a beat. Then she shoved the model canoe into Moana's hands. "Well, then I can do better than this."

Moana smiled and turned to leave at the same time that Loto used her adze to sever a rope above her head. A log whizzed by, narrowly missing her.

As Moana left the boathouse, her heart pounding from the narrow escape, she smiled. Picking Loto had been a no-brainer. Loto's inventive skills would be invaluable on the journey. But there were a few other things her crew would need, too. Next stop, the fields.

She found Kele right where she'd expected. The grumpy elderly farmer was tending a crop of taro plants. He wasn't particularly nice to people, but he loved his plants and was an expert at making them grow. He was delicately patting the dirt around one of them now, a picture of patience. But as soon as Moana told him why she was there—to add a farmer to her crew—his shoulders hunched and the scowl on his face grew even more severe.

"A *farmer* on the *sea?*" he ranted.

Moana nodded, taking a bite out of the banana that Kele's overeager apprentice had handed her. "We'll need to eat more than fish—"

Kele cut her off. "You'd need irrigation, plant propagation," he explained. Then he pointed to his apprentice. "Take even my best apprentice—you'd starve."

Moana bit back a smile. "Exactly," she said, leading Kele into her trap. "We need a master."

"Yes, you do need—"

Those were exactly the words she needed to hear. This time it was Moana who cut him off. "Thanks, Kele!" she said in a singsong voice before bolting off. Behind her she heard him grumbling. But she wasn't going give him the chance to take it back.

Her crew was almost complete.

A short while later, Moana slipped into the storytelling fale. It was quiet—the children were out playing.

She approached the siapo of Maui that hung on one wall. His muscled form seemed to fill up the room, as if he were about to jump off the fabric at any moment and start teasing her. If only. She really wished he were joining her on this voyage. She missed her friend.

"Maui," she said softly. "It's been a while. I don't know where you are, but I could really use your help."

She startled as a shadowy figure that looked like Maui appeared behind the siapo. Could it be? "Maui!" she cried. Excited, she pulled back the siapo.

It was Moni.

The village's historian stepped out from behind the siapo, broadly smiling. "Actually, it's both of us," he said, missing that Moana had thought the actual demigod had answered her plea. He pulled out several more siapos and lined them up. "Maui *and* me. It's part of a series."

Moana's eyes flew over the siapos that did, indeed, depict the pair in different scenes. She had to admit, the images were pretty great. Both the demigod and the historian were undeniably strong. Together on the siapos, they looked ready to take on anything.

"It's too bad Maui isn't here," Moni went on. "You really need someone who knows all the old stories and, you know, is superstrong, and has great hair."

Moana nodded, looking back and forth between the image of Maui and Moni the person. "I mean, I know someone else kinda like that. . . ." She let her thought trail off, hoping Moni would get what she was hinting at.

He didn't.

She waited, giving him another moment. Then she nodded at the siapo and back at him. She raised her eyebrows.

Finally, Moni got it. *"Really?"* he cried. "Yes! I'm going with Moana on a call from the ancestors! Get ready for some eyewitness accounts!"

Eyewitness accounts would be great. But having

someone who knew all the stories about angry gods being beaten would be invaluable. And the fact that he was pretty strong didn't hurt.

Moana smiled. She had her crew.

Moana's canoe was in the water. The crew was ready. Moana just needed to load the last basket and they could set sail. But when she went to lift the basket, she couldn't. It was too heavy.

She peeked inside. Simea stared up at her with big, pleading eyes. "I'm going with you," she said, trying to sound tough but failing as her voice quivered.

Tears pricked Moana's eyes. She had been so busy finding her crew and packing the canoe, she hadn't had the time to think about this—the hardest goodbye of all. But now there was no time left.

The sadness in her sister's eyes made her heart break. "I'll be back as soon as I can," she said, lifting Simea out of the basket. "I promise."

"What if you *don't* come back?" Simea asked. Fear was written all over her face.

Moana swallowed. How could she reassure her sister

when she was so unsure herself? It felt impossible. But then her eyes drifted out toward the water. She had an idea.

Taking Simea's hand, she led the little girl down to a secluded part of the lagoon. She stepped into the water, made golden by the rising sun. Leaning down, she twirled her fingers in it.

"The ocean is my friend," she said. "*Our* friend. It connects us. So there is nowhere I could ever go that I won't be with you."

Simea followed the ripples in the water as they moved away from them. Then, realizing what her sister meant, she nodded. Picking up a sea star, she placed it in Moana's necklace. "So you can take a piece from home."

Moana smiled, tears in her eyes. And when Simea threw her arms around her waist, she hugged back as hard as she could. It was a hug, she hoped, that would last until she returned.

When she finally pulled away, the sun was higher in the sky. She didn't have any more time. She and her crew had to get going while the comet was still there to guide them.

With Simea following, Moana made her way back to the canoe. The whole village had gathered to see her and her crew off. As she approached, they parted, creating a path for her to walk through.

At the end of the path stood her mother and father. Beyond them, her canoe bobbed in the water. Loto, Kele, and Moni were already aboard. As the villagers continued to call out their well-wishes, Moana hugged her family.

She was silent. There was nothing left to say.

Then, with a tight squeeze, she turned and hopped up on the canoe to join her crew. Pua lifted the sail line with his nose, and she gave him a thankful nod. Of course he was coming along. As was Heihei. At least one of them might be helpful. The villagers let out a cheer as the sail opened. In the center was an image of the island of Motufetū with the constellation above it.

Moana steered the canoe into the open water. Turning, she waved one last time. And then, as the cheers faded and the wind picked up, Moana looked ahead. The comet shone brightly, even in the morning sky.

Her course was set.

It was time to find Motufetū.

CHAPTER 7

Maui was having a bad day. Actually, he was having a lot of bad days. How many, exactly? He had no way to tell. It was hard to gauge the passing of time while stuck in a dark windowless space that smelled like something between rotting eggs and decaying fish. Which was, unfortunately, where Maui currently found himself.

If that wasn't bad enough, he was dangling at the end of a rope in the middle of the dark space, his body wrapped up in a giant fish skeleton, which was tied several times around his body, pinning his arms to his sides. He could barely move except to sway his body slightly.

And while all that wasn't great and the stink was downright awful, the worst part was that the rope he was dangling from was connected to Maui's own hook. His hook was attached to a separate rope that seemed to disappear into the endless darkness above.

But despite all that, Maui held his head high as he spoke. His voice echoed off distant walls. "One more time," he said defiantly. Then louder: "This is not the end of our story! This is not where our destiny is denied. Together we rise as one! Together we take our freedom!"

He looked down, hoping his speech had inspired the gathered crowd—the crowd, in this case, being a large pile of mudskippers. The slimy, bug-eyed fish stared blankly at Maui.

Maui frowned. But then he saw one of the mudskippers slowly look up—right at him! "*That* guy gets it!" he said, feeling a glimmer of hope. "Yup, I mean you, handsome. Now all ya gotta do is get my hook!"

On Maui's chest, Mini Maui shook his head. This

never worked. They had tried many, many times. The mudskippers had never moved.

Until now!

Slowly, the fish began to pile on top of each other, forming a sort of mudskipper pyramid. Were they actually trying to reach Maui's hook?

"Ha! Yes! That's what I'm talking about!" Maui said, feeling triumphant. "Higher! Higher! Almost there, just a little high—" His voice trailed off as a gurgling noise sounded from somewhere above him. The mudskippers paused, too. "Whoa, no! Don't stop! Just keep going!"

The gurgling, squelching noise grew louder. Before the fish pyramid could reach the hook, another noise—almost like a burp—erupted, and a moment later, a waterfall of half-eaten fish and kelp washed away the pile of mudskippers.

Maui, his hair dripping in sea mush, sighed. On Maui's shoulder, Mini Maui drew a new tally mark next to the dozens already there.

"Don't worry," Maui said, trying to sound convincing. "I'll get us out of here."

Mini Maui pointed to the tattoo of Moana, as if suggesting that perhaps she could help.

Maui looked offended at the suggestion. He was a

demigod. "No, I don't need her to save me . . ." After a look from Mini Maui, he went on. ". . . again. 'Cause she'll die. Nalo hates humans even more than he hates me. And, uh, he hates me a lot."

Mini Maui nodded. That was an understatement.

"So the farther Curly is from any of this, the better." He maneuvered his body, causing the rope to swing. "We're on our own." Then he got an idea. He grabbed the rope with his teeth. He would chew his way out if he had to!

Sensing someone—or something—Maui paused. Slowly, he looked up. Immediately, he wished he hadn't. Matangi was hovering above him. She must have been there the whole time, enjoying watching him struggle. Maui snarled.

"Hmm, I would let you out, but . . . ," said Matangi. Then her voice changed, turning sickly sweet. "I'm *really* hoping to meet your little friend. I have plans for you both."

"What?" Maui shouted as Matangi faded from view. "Hey! HEY!"

But it was no use.

She was gone.

There was another burping noise. More sea mush poured down on him.

Maui frowned. He was going to need to wash his hair as soon as he got out of there. *If* he got out of there.

He really hoped Moana was faring better than this . . . wherever she was.

CHAPTER 8

Moana was up at the top of the mast, tracking the comet in the distance. It was a beautiful sight. She inhaled the fresh ocean air. Checking her necklace, she glanced at the sea star tucked inside to ensure it was where it belonged.

Bock!

Out of nowhere, Heihei surprised Moana with a peck right on her nose.

"Ow, you gotta stop doing that," Moana said. "Whoa!" The mast bobbled. Moana looked down and saw Loto chopping it with her adze!

"Loto? What are you doing?" Moana asked.

"Making improvements!" Loto explained. "Heihei gave me an idea!"

Moana zipped down the mast. "Okay, you gotta get outta your head. The canoe is perfect as it is."

"Perfection's a myth. There is only failing, then learning, then death," replied Loto.

Before Moana could respond, the canoe began to turn . . . away from the comet.

Moni was supposed to be steering. Instead, he was painting a siapo of Moana leading the voyage.

"Moni!" she shouted as the canoe swerved off course. "The oar!"

But he was oblivious. He added an oar to the image he was painting. "Of course! That's why you're the wayfinder."

Moana sighed. She adjusted their path to continue following the comet.

WHACK!

Loto sliced a rope, moving the sail. As the canoe unexpectedly pivoted again, the entire crew slid across the boat. Moana quickly fixed their path again.

"Guys, this is an epic voyage," she said. "Let's take it all in, stay on course, and keep everyone on the canoe."

She quickly did a head count. They were down one. "Wait, where's the farmer? Where's Kele!"

At that moment, Pua, dazed from sliding, stumbled past her and into the cargo hold.

"OW!"

Moana's eyes narrowed. She leaned over and peered into the hold to find Kele. The farmer was covering his eyes. "When will the canoe stop *moving*?" he groaned.

"Well, we're kinda on the ocean," Moana said, teasing him slightly. "How 'bout some fresh air?" she said, offering her hand to hoist him out of the cargo hold.

"A worm prefers his dirt," Kele replied as he lifted a handful of dirt from a pot and sniffed it like a child sniffing their blankie.

Just then, the canoe swung wildly this time. Moni wasn't paying attention—again. Moana went flying, clawing at the deck to keep from falling off.

Getting to her feet, she scrambled to right the ship and get them back on course. "Guys!" she shouted to the crew. "We'll never make it if you don't embrace the ocean!"

"Can't embrace a liquid," replied Loto.

"Also, I cannot swim," Kele pointed out.

This was not going to do. Moana needed to get

them excited. "We wanna reach Motufetū?" she said. The others eyed her skeptically. "We gotta enjoy it. Breathe it in, live in the moment."

Her words echoed over the waves. On the canoe, the crew was silent.

Moana sighed. The wind, the sea, the sky, nothing was better than this. How did her crew not feel the same way?

This was going to take some time.

Luckily, they had plenty of it.

With each passing day, Moana tried to encourage the crew to embrace the ocean and realize how special this journey they shared was. She wanted them to feel like she felt about the adventure.

Through pounding rain, a scary lightning storm, and burning hot and freezing cold conditions, the crew worked together and kept the comet in their sights. Many times they wanted to give up. The task at hand felt too perilous, but somehow they survived.

Eventually, they sailed past Te Fiti. They had arrived in new territory.

With each difficulty they encountered along the

way, the crew slowly began to see Moana's point of view.

Kele started to tolerate the sea. Moni found new scenes to depict that were unlike anything he had painted in the past. Loto stopped randomly cutting things down. Even Pua and Heihei settled into a routine. None of them could sail the canoe, but at least now they were comfortable on it.

All the while, Moana kept the canoe moving forward, following the path of the comet. Occasionally, she would trace the outline of the shell Simea had given her in the ocean, sending a silent message across the waves to her sister. The ocean always answered, bringing Simea's messages to her in the way of splashes and a face full of water. But Moana didn't mind. It made her heart happy to know that the ocean remained her friend, that her sister was okay, that her crew was working together, and that the comet was showing them the way.

But at that moment, the comet began to sputter. It flamed brightly.

Then it disappeared.

"Isn't that what we were supposed to follow?" Kele asked after a moment of stunned silence.

Moana, her wide eyes desperately scanning the empty

sky, said, "Uh, let's . . . Nobody panic. . . ." She was definitely panicking. "I'm sure this happened for a reason. It's probably a good thing."

WHOOSH!

The canoe suddenly lurched in the opposite direction, sending the crew flying. Moana glanced around. What just happened?

"Moni, grab the oar!" she called.

Leaping up, Moni rushed over to the large steering oar and began to help Moana try to move it. But the oar wouldn't budge. The canoe wouldn't change course.

"I'm trying! Something's wrong with the canoe!" Moni said through gritted teeth as he continued to push at the oar.

"It is *not* my canoe," Loto defensively retorted. "It is the current."

Moana needed help. The ocean had helped her on her last adventure. Maybe it would help her now.

"Hey, Ocean," she whispered, leaning over the edge of the canoe and speaking to the rushing water. "So I kinda wasn't given a lot of directions. So, uhhh, if this is your way of telling me to change course, a little thumbs-up would be super awesome."

As if in response, the canoe sped up, pulled by the mysterious current.

Moana was confused. Was that a thumbs-up? Had the ocean even heard her?

Before she could figure it out, Kele called, "Land? Land!"

Moana squinted into the sun. There *was* something on the horizon. And the strong current was bringing them closer.

"It's Motufetū!" Moni said, his voice full of awe. "We found it! Mission accomplished!"

"Do I hear *people*?" Loto asked.

Sure enough, there was the sound of indistinct chattering coming over the waves. While the others began to smile, Moana frowned. Something wasn't right. This had been too easy. If Motufetū was so simple to find, one of her ancestors would have found it ages ago.

Her heart sank as the "island" came into view.

It was a barge.

"That's no island. And those aren't people," Moana said.

They hadn't found Motufetū.

The Kakamora had found *them*.

CHAPTER 9

Moana and her crew watched as the huge Kakamora barge came out of the fog. It was just like the one she had encountered with Maui. Only this one was bigger. Much bigger. And when the Kakamora extended their sails, it was also much faster.

That was when they heard the Kakamora's war cry.

As the barge picked up speed and barreled toward them, Moana sprang into action. "So, I don't want to panic everyone," she said as she rushed around the canoe. "But if the Kakamora catch us, they will . . . kinda, sorta, definitely kill us. Go, team!"

That snapped the crew out of their stupor. But instead of helping Moana, they scattered in a panic. Above their own frantic cries came the sound of the Kakamora's war cry again. There had to be hundreds of the coconut-shaped creatures.

The barge came closer and closer. Moana gulped. There was no way they could escape. She didn't have Maui. Her crew wasn't ready. They had nowhere to go.

Beside her, Kele had the same thought. "Disgraceful," he muttered. "A farmer, murdered by coconuts."

They collectively sucked in their breaths.

This was it.

Death was inevitable.

Then the barge raced right past them!

Well, that was weird, Moana thought.

"Guess we were scared for nothing," Moni said aloud, turning back to his friends.

But why would the Kakamora not attack them? Were they fleeing something?

Moana's thoughts trailed off as she looked ahead and saw *exactly* what had scared the Kakamora. A huge, monstrous clam was sucking the ocean into its gaping maw! That was what had created the current that pulled them so quickly to the Kakamora!

Anything that got in the clam's way, or was pulled

to it on the current, was immediately eaten. Moana watched in horror as it chomped down on another, smaller Kakamora barge that hadn't been able to escape.

"I think I know what's causing the current," said Loto, stating the obvious.

They needed to get out of it, fast.

"You guys, cargo hold!" she cried, pushing her stunned crew down into the small space. With them safely out of the way, she got to work. Grabbing a pile of rope in one hand and the oar in the other, she steered the canoe into the wake of the fleeing Kakamora barge. She let the canoe steady itself. When the moment was right, she threw the rope. It swung high before snagging on the barge and going taut. Her canoe was propelled forward—right around the barge!

Moana heard Loto's impressed gasp. "Whoa! By adjusting our trajectory, she's using centrifugal force to increase our velocity."

Moana hadn't really thought about the science behind it, but either way, Loto was right. They were going faster by the second. They quickly flew in front of the Kakamora barge. Now it, not them, was in position to get sucked up by the massive clam.

Confident that they were in the clear, Moana turned and gave the Kakamora a sassy wave. "Buh-bye!" she called out in a singsong voice, preparing to cut the rope and free her canoe. "Thanks for the ride—"

A loud, ominous creaking sound made Moana cringe. As she watched, the rope connecting the canoe to the Kakamora barge snagged on a reef hidden beneath the water. The rope pulled tight and then swung the two boats into each other. There was a sickening thud as they collided. Then silence.

They were stuck with a bargeful of angry coconuts who had a history of blowing tranquilizer darts at anyone who got in their way.

Moana didn't know which was worse. This, or being sucked up by a giant clam.

Making sure the crew was still in the hold, Moana grabbed her oar. She wouldn't go down without a fight. "Bring it on, Coco—"

Thwip, thwip, thwip.

Kakamora darts sank into her back. "Nuts," she said, before falling to the ground.

Moana's bones felt like jelly. Her hands and feet were tied, which seemed a bit unnecessary. She wanted to move and fight, but she could barely hold her head up.

The rest of her crew were in no better shape, except for Heihei, who somehow seemed to be unaffected.

"Don't worry, guysh. I'll git ush outta dish—" she said, struggling to make her mouth work. While she couldn't see most of the Kakamora, she could sense them all around her. And from the sound of their chattering, they were pretty angry. Maybe she could reason with them?

"Hey! Hey! Listen to me! We are on a shacred voyage. You will releash us—" It was no use. She didn't sound authoritative. She sounded ridiculous.

A pecking noise nearby distracted her. With great effort, she moved her head and saw Heihei. The rooster was pecking at the rope connected to the canoe's sail. Suddenly, there was a ripping noise and the rope snapped, releasing the sail. As the wind filled it, the image of the island of Motufetū with the constellation above revealed itself.

Everything went silent.

Then the Kakamora began to cheer wildly.

Moana and her crew were aboard the Kakamora barge while all the Kakamora continued their celebration.

Well, not *all* of them were celebrating. There was one particularly surly coconut named Kotu who kept giving her the stink eye. He was the chief's son. Cranky must have run in the family.

"What ish happening?" Moana asked. Nothing about this made sense.

The others agreed. They were completely baffled.

Suddenly, one of the Kakamora approached Moni. He held up one of Moni's siapos. Unfurling it, he nodded at the image of Maui and Moni fighting the Kakamora and winning. The Kakamora pointed at the siapo, then at Moni, and then back at the siapo as if to say, *Did you draw this?*

Moni nodded proudly. "That is . . . fanfic," he said.

Beside him, Kele groaned. Being shot by a tranquilizer dart had not made his surly attitude any less surly. "You dolt. They're ashking if you drew it 'caushe they want you to transhlate that picture," he said.

The Kakamora gathered in front of them. They began to maneuver themselves into shapes, like a simple picture made of dots. Moana watched, trying to figure out what they were doing. But Moni somehow knew right away. They were showing them the Kakamora history.

"Oh— *Oh,* uh, your home island is in the same sea

as Motufetū." As he translated, the Kakamora continue to move, revealing new images. "And when Nalo cursed it, the ocean channels leading there disappeared. And your ancestors couldn't find their way home. But you thought you'd finally found a path, until you ran into this giant clam and now you're worried you'll be stuck forever and never fulfill your ancestors' dreams," His voice trailed off as he looked over at the Kakamora chief. The chief nodded, confirming that Moni's interpretation was correct.

Moana looked back and forth between Moni and the Kakamora. "This whole time, they've just been trying to get home?" They wanted the same thing! Moana realized she had more in common with the Kakamora than she'd thought.

The chief pointed to Moana and the crew. Then he gestured to the giant clam. Moana understood his offer.

"But if we help you defeat the clam, you'll help us reach Motufetū . . . together," she said.

The chief nodded.

Kele interrupted the moment. "Hello! We're still jelly!" He gestured toward Moana. "How're we gonna beat that? Floppy can't even wiggle a finger."

"Well, her muscles *are* full of neurotoxin," Loto explained. Then her face lit up. "Wait, hang on! A clam

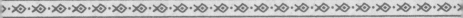

is basically one giant muscle. We get close enough to shoot it in the ganglion, it's lights-out paralysis for the clam and *hello,* Motufetū."

Moana tried her best to give Loto a smile of approval. Her team was coming through! Then she raised her eyes back to the chief. "You want us to do it," she said. "Can you make us *not* jelly?"

CHAPTER 10

Moana stared at the giant, disgusting blobfish in front of her. The gelatinous creature stared back. Or at least, Moana thought so. It was kind of hard to tell. *This* was how they were going to get un-jellied?

Apparently, yes.

Holding back a gag, Moana felt the blobfish sliding over her body, covering her in goo. One by one, the crew met the same fate, until the blobfish goo covered all of them, leaving them completely nauseated.

But when the toxin removal was finished, Moana

could sit up—on her own. Sure, she was still covered in slime, but it had worked!

"Okay!" she said, wiping a glob of slime off her face. "Where do we get the toxin for the clam?"

At that very moment, the blobfish sneezed out the toxin. In a practiced move, the Kakamora held up a vat, catching the goo.

"A dream from both ends," Loto said, genuinely impressed.

Moana didn't have time to decide how she felt about this. Beneath them, the barge shifted and the reef groaned. The reef was about to break apart. They were running out of time.

Racing to the deck of the barge, she swung down onto her canoe and began to ready it. She pulled ropes, tied down equipment, and stowed Heihei—not that that had ever done much good.

"C'mon!" she shouted to the others. "We gotta go!"

On the barge, the Kakamora began to bang their drums. Then Kotu ziplined down onto the canoe. Dipping an arrow into a bowl of neurotoxin, he held it out to Moana. She reached for it. He didn't let go.

Beneath them, the reef cracked again. It was going to completely disintegrate at any moment.

Kotu didn't trust her. She didn't blame him. After all, she did battle them once before.

"We *made* a deal. We take out the clam and then you're helping us get to Motufetū. I got it."

For a moment, Moana wondered if Kotu was going to continue being stubborn. But then he reluctantly handed over the arrow. His duty done, he launched himself back up onto the barge and took his spot beside the chief.

"I don't think he likes us," said Kele, stating the obvious. "Us meaning *you*."

Loosening the ropes that attached the canoe to the barge, the Kakamora sent Moana and her crew on their way. They would remain attached by the rope so that when it was time, the Kakamora could pull the canoe back to safety. At least, that was the plan.

From somewhere behind them, the clam let out a growl. Moana took one last look up at the barge. The chief met her gaze. As the canoe drifted from the reef, the chief began to tap out a rhythmic beat on his shell.

"It's a warriors' salute," Moni said, realizing. Up on the barge, all the Kakamora joined in. "Or they're saying goodbye in case we, *you know*. That part's unclear."

The clam let out another terrible roar. A gust of wind whooshed past the crew. Moana took a deep breath, reaching for her necklace. She thought of Simea and exhaled. She steadied herself, knowing she had the strength to hold up her side of the deal.

Within moments of leaving the reef, they were sucked between the two sides of the clam's mouth. The stench was nearly unbearable, and strange, thin tendrils slithered around them.

"Don't touch the feelers," Loto said, nodding to the tendrils. "I'll trigger the clam to shut. I think. Or we *could* test it."

Everyone, even Pua and Heihei, shook their heads. "No!" they cried. This was not the time for Loto to test her hypothesis.

Kele frowned. "How do we shoot the"—he struggled for the word—"'ganglion' if we don't know what it looks like?"

Moni shrugged. "I'll bet we'll know when we see it," he answered.

As if on cue, a small bump appeared above them. It didn't look particularly scary. It was actually cute, with pretty little bioluminescent lights pointing to what appeared to be its center. Like a bull's-eye.

The team looked at each other. *This* was the ganglion?

"So I just"—Moana held up her spear and mimed

jabbing it at the ganglion—"and it's Motufetū, here we come?" It seemed almost easy.

Too easy.

Just then, there was a loud creaking sound from outside the clam. The reef was giving way! It yanked the barge as it started to split. The canoe, which was still tied to the barge, swerved. Struggling to keep her footing, Moana lost hold of the spear. She let out a cry as it fell into the abyss of the clam's maw.

"No, no, no!" Moana shouted.

"And *this* is why you always have a backup!" Loto said, pulling out another spear. She grinned—until Heihei fell right on top of her. The second spear vanished. But Loto wasn't worried. She held up another. "*And* a third!"

WHAM!

This time, Kele tumbled into Loto. The third and final spear joined the others.

As the reef continued to break apart, Moana looked around. There had to be a way out of this mess. And then she spotted it! One of the spears hadn't been lost to the depths of the ocean. It had lodged itself on something below her. Leaning over the edge of the canoe, she struggled to reach it. But she couldn't get close enough.

Just then, ziplining from the barge to the canoe, Kotu flew into the clam's maw. *Thwip!* He fired off a massive, toxin-filled spear. It hit the ganglion and exploded, covering the bump with toxin. The clam began to gurgle and spasm.

He had done it!

But the clam's shuddering cracked the reef completely, causing the Kakamora barge to be sucked toward the clam. At the same time, the clam's mouth was shutting.

"Guys! We gotta get out! Pull the rope!" Moana yelled.

Moana's eyes met Kotu's. She made a promise to herself to return him to his family when this all was behind them.

Frantically, Moana tugged at the rope with all her strength, trying to pull them free of the clam's mouth. Kotu joined. But it was no use. They weren't strong enough.

The rope was straining under the intense pull of their canoe as the waters inside raged, pulling the Kakamora barge with it. If they didn't release the barge, it would be sucked inside the clam along with their canoe.

Kotu looked out at the barge. Then back at the rope.

Moana knew what he was going to do. He was

going to sacrifice them to save his family. "No! No don't! Stop!"

With one final look at the barge, Kotu used his knife to sever the rope. It was the crew's only chance of being saved.

With an intense *whoosh,* they were pulled into a whirlpool of water forming inside the clam.

Then the monstrous creature swallowed them whole.

CHAPTER 11

Maui knew it was only a matter of time before being trapped in this dark, stinky prison would make him go mad. Even demigods had a limit. And apparently he had reached his, because he could have sworn he heard humans screaming.

The screaming, if in fact there was any screaming at all, also appeared to be getting louder. As if whatever humans were making the noise were falling fast toward him. He cocked his head. A moment later, there was a thud, and he was falling. Maui landed on the slimy ground. Hard.

"Oh, yeah!" Maui cried. He had no idea what had just happened, but he didn't care. Sure, his body was still bound by the fish bones and rope, but he felt like he'd already escaped.

He glanced down at Mini Maui. "Oh, yeah! Told ya I'd get us out!"

Since his hands were still pinned at his sides, he couldn't use them to push his body to a standing position. So after taking a deep breath, he arched his back, and with a mighty heave, he went from lying down to standing. When he was back on his feet, he shook out his hair. Or at least, tried to. It was hard when it was caked with sea goo.

Lifting his head, he saw his hook dangling above him. The rope he used to be suspended from lay on the ground just out of reach. If he could get the rope, he could lasso the hook and pull himself up to it. And then he'd be out of there!

The only problem was that his arms were still bound at his sides. Cracking his neck, he shimmied his body back and forth. He stretched and strained as far as he could, trying to reach the rope, groaning from the effort. Finally, he felt the rope with his fingertips! Almost there. . . .

"Maui????????"

A human's face appeared, scaring the demigod. With a cry, he let go of the rope. The movement sent him rocking back, and once again, he found himself lying on the floor. Only this time, he began to roll around the cavernous room. He came to a stop on his back, like a turtle. On his chest, Mini Maui shook his head.

Loto, Kele, and Moni stared down at him.

"The tattoo moves!" Moni cried. "The tattoo moves!"

Next to him, Loto narrowed her eyes. Then, carefully reaching through the fish bones surrounding Maui's chest, she poked Mini Maui.

"Hey, stop that!" Maui said. "Just stop it. I am a demigod." As he spoke, he rolled himself upright. "Okay, rule number one . . ." His body shifted. He rolled back onto his side. This was not going well. "Just, okay. Someone roll me back. Roll me back!"

"*I'll* roll you back!" Moni said with a little too much excitement.

Maui frowned. He wasn't sure he liked the enthusiasm behind the offer. Or the way that Moni was staring at him. Of course, he was used to humans staring. But this went a bit beyond the usual starstruck ogling. "Not you! Not him!"

Thankfully, Loto was willing to help. Behind her, Kele leaned over to Moni. "This is what happens when you meet your heroes," he said, sounding deeply unimpressed by the presence of Maui and his inability to keep his body in one place.

But Kele's sarcasm was lost on Moni. "I know, right?" Moni said, clearly enraptured.

Maui took a deep breath and tried again. "Rule number one," he said. "You never saw me like this. Even though I still look very cool."

"You look like a kidney stone," replied Kele.

"And you look like someone who would know what that is," Maui quipped. "Now, I don't know how you three got here and I don't care. . . ."

Just then, Kotu climbed out of a pile of trash. Maui hadn't seen that coming.

A moment later, Pua came loose from somewhere above and fell onto Maui's head. He bounced off Maui and landed on the ground. Pua? He had not seen that coming either. "Well, hello, Bacon," he said, eyeing the pig hungrily. Then he turned to the humans. There was definitely a backstory he needed to get caught up on. And he wasn't sure why they had Moana's pig. But right now he had some serious demigod stuff to handle.

Once again grabbing the rope, Maui threw it toward the hook. The toss was awkward because his arms were still pinned to his sides by the rope and fish bones, but he somehow managed to lasso his hook. With a mighty heave, he pulled it down. He let out a happy cheer before giving the hook a kiss. It was good to have it back.

"Be back in a bit," he told the others. "Decade, tops."

With a gleeful *Chee Hoo!,* he transformed—into a bug. The rope and fish bones around his body fell to the ground in a pile and he zoomed away, finally free. He transformed again into several different animals in quick succession, then finally returned to the demigod Maui.

Glancing over, he saw the awestruck look on the others' faces. He smiled. *Still got it,* he mused. He started to leave but thought better of it. He should at least give them some advice first. "Stay alive, talk to no one," he warned. "And if ya see a crazy bat lady, run. She's the worst. Full of lies . . . and bats. In that order. And she will trap you in her web, like a spider." The humans looked terrified. "But to be clear, she is not a spider. But she *is* a liar. Who traps people. Actually, she should probably have spiders instead of bats. . . ." He felt a pinch and looked down. Mini Maui was signaling for him to wrap it up.

Moni's mouth opened and closed, as if he wanted to

ask a question but didn't know where to begin. Maui had no time for that. "Point is, stay away or you will die. Be good!"

He was turning to go when a nearby mudskipper began to flop around oddly. There was a *cluck,* and out of its mouth popped Heihei!

"Boat snack!" Maui said, oddly happy to see the rooster. *But wait,* he thought. *What is Heihei doing here? And, come to think of it, why is Pua here, too?* He looked down at Mini Maui, horror coming over him.

"Where's Moana?"

Moana looked out at the calm waters of Motunui. Beneath her feet, the sand was warm. She was home? But how was that possible? Had she been sucked into a weird portal when the clam swallowed them? Stranger things *had* happened. . . .

"Moana!"

Turning at the familiar voice, she got a huge smile on her face. Simea!

"Simea? Simea! How are you here?" Moana said, tightly squeezing her sister.

Her sister squeezed back. "I'm not," she said in a

voice that was sweet. Too sweet. "You got sucked inside a giant clam and you let everyone down and now you'll never finish what Tautai Vasa started and reconnect the people of the ocean and your ancestors will be like 'Moana, we hate you forever. . . .'"

A strange flapping noise filled Moana's ears.

Moana pulled back, confused. She stared in horror as "Simea" sprouted bat ears. Fear flooded her as she watched her sister transform in front of her eyes. . . .

Moana woke with a start. A bat was staring down at her. Instinctively, she reached with one hand for her shell necklace and jumped up and grabbed her oar with the other. She began to swing her oar at the bat, but the creature just latched on and refused to let go.

Finally, the bat released its grip. Moana let out a sigh of relief. It was short-lived, as suddenly hundreds of bats swarmed around her. Moana swatted at them to try to make a path in the darkness, but it was no use. There were just too many of them. "I got this. I *got* this," she said, trying to psych herself up as more bats seemed to swarm her.

To her surprise, someone replied.

"You got this."

Moana spun toward the voice, and the bat storm

dissipated. She found herself staring at a beautiful, purple-eyed demigod. She was hanging upside down from a siapo cloth. Despite the fear filling her body, Moana couldn't help being impressed.

"Relax, I don't bite," the demigod said. She nodded at the bat Moana had first tried to remove from her oar. "Peka might." Shrugging, she slid farther down the siapo before flipping over and landing gracefully on her feet. Slowly, she walked around Moana, sizing her up.

Moana lifted her chin. She wasn't going to let this demigod, whoever she was, intimidate her.

"Been a while since I've seen a wayfinder." She gestured at Moana. "The uniform. Necklace. Oar."

Moana lifted her oar like a weapon. "Would you like to see me use it?"

"Oh, feisty! We have that in common . . . Moana." At Moana's surprised look, the demigod nodded. "The human who's got all the gods talking! I thought you'd be more . . . *more.*"

She began to slide in and out of Moana's vision, dipping into the shadows. But Moana refused to participate in this demigod's game. Every minute she was here with . . . well, whoever this was, was a minute she wasn't tracking down her crew and Motufetū. Next time the demigod sidled by, Moana's oar whipped out, pinning the demigod's siapo. "Who *are* you?" Moana demanded.

"Matangi," the demigod replied. She eyed Moana with new interest. "Guardian of this little slice of paradise."

Moana looked around at the rather uninspiring surroundings. "You *live* here?"

"Not by choice," Matangi replied. Then she frowned. "Maui never mentioned me? Funny, he said so much with so *little* about you."

Moana's heart quickened. "Hey. stop. You've seen Maui?" she said, unable to hide the hope in her voice. "Is he . . . Wait, is he here?"

Matangi didn't answer Moana's question. "So much to learn," she replied cryptically. "Come on, then."

Matangi disappeared only to reappear on a skiff. The small boat seemed to float on fog. A sail had been fashioned into a hammock, and Matangi lay in the middle. She gestured for Moana to join her.

Moana shook her head. "I'm not going anywhere with you," she said. "I need to—"

Matangi finished for her. "Get outta here, break Nalo's curse, find Motufetū . . ." The smile that spread across Matangi's face seemed threatening. "Here to help."

Moana's eyes were wide. How had Matangi known all that? And what else did she know?

Moana couldn't help herself, despite the uneasy sense that filled her body. "You know the way to Motufetū"?

Matangi sighed, as though disappointed by Moana's question. "You think you can only get somewhere if you know the way?"

"That's kinda what wayfinding is," Moana replied.

"Ugh, just when I was starting to buy the hype. A *true* wayfinder has no idea where they're going. That's the whole point. Finding your way to what's never been found. If you wanna succeed, you gotta go off the charts, sis. Get a little lost."

As Moana watched, the skiff suddenly took off in the opposite direction. It zoomed onto the ceiling and raced over her head. Flipping itself back over, it sped straight toward Moana. Just before it crashed into her, Matangi reached out and grabbed Moana, pulling her aboard.

"Why should I listen to anything you say?" Moana asked. She glanced over her shoulder. Hopefully she would remember a way to get back there when this— whatever it was—was over.

"Because until you break the curse, I can't get out," Matangi replied as she circled Moana. "So I'm the best thing that could've happened to you."

As the skiff shot through the dark space, Matangi continued. For Moana to find her way, she explained, first she would have to get lost.

Moana was determined to keep her bearings, no matter how hard Matangi tried to disorient her . . . which she was trying very hard to do.

"A true wayfinder has no idea where they're going; that's the whole point," Matangi said, echoing her advice from before. "To find your way to what's never been found."

Moana frowned. She still had no idea what Matangi meant, but right now she had no other choice but to try to understand. Despite the freaky bats and the purple eyes, she got the sense that the demigod might know what she was talking about.

Beneath them, the skiff moved swiftly along an underground river. Up ahead, Moana saw a fork in their path. One way led to calm waters, and the other appeared to drop off into a dark void. Matangi was steering them toward the dark void!

Grabbing her oar, Moana maneuvered the skiff until they were aimed at the calm path. Then she suddenly

realized, as the water grew white and rough, that it wasn't so calm after all. Moana let out a shout as they went over a waterfall. Just before she fell, Matangi reached out and grabbed her, saving her.

Matangi placed Moana in a giant shell and spun her, disorienting her even more. When it finally came to a stop, Moana found herself back at the same fork in the river. Moana was faced with the same choice: stay on the path and go over the falls again or brave the scarier-looking option in the fork. *What's down that path?* Moana wondered. There was only one way to find out.

She paddled with all her might into the darkness.

Then she fell.

And it was thrilling!

Moana was definitely lost. She was surrounded by roiling, swirling purple clouds without any sense of direction. It was impossible to see anything but that she was trapped inside a giant pearl with no way out. She could feel panic creeping in.

Taking a deep breath, Moana centered herself. Maybe Matangi hadn't tricked her. Moana began to spin her oar around and around, creating a whirlpool of clouds. Faster and faster she went until, with a *whoosh,* she could see the floor beneath her.

Moana gasped. She was standing on a huge, carved face. And not just any face, but one that looked just like the one Maui had opened when they went to Lalotai to retrieve his hook. It was a way out! Matangi had helped her!

BOOM!

Maui, along with the rest of Moana's crew, came flying into the cavern with her canoe. But Moana couldn't see them through the dark-purple clouds.

A moment later, Matangi appeared as well.

"Moana?" Maui said, turning his hook toward Matangi. "Let her out!"

As though Moana could hear her friend's command, she pulled the words Maui had said that day in Lalotai from her memory. She began to chant as she stomped her feet on the carved face inside the pearl. Her stomping grew harder, her words louder, and then there was another boom and the pearlescent wall around her exploded, sending shimmering sparks through the air. The mouth of the carved face had opened! It was a door.

Moana looked around her in awe.

"Maui?" she shouted.

The two friends looked at each other, stunned. But

there was no time for a reunion. The swirling fog and smoke from inside the pearl began to envelope the entire room. A light glowed around them. Moana had opened a portal.

"You know, I think you need her as much as she needs you," Matangi said.

The smoke swirled around everyone. Maui's and Moana's crew were sucked into the portal, leaving Moana behind.

Moana locked eyes with Matangi. It was a moment of mutual respect.

"Well, good luck, wayfinder," said Matangi. "Don't mess it up."

Then Moana disappeared into the portal.

It felt like she was falling in slow motion. Time felt suspended. She heard odd, distorted voices behind her. As she moved through the space, a kaleidoscope of colors appeared and disappeared.

Then, with another *whoosh*, Moana was shot out of the portal and into a swirling tunnel. Time seemed to resume its normal speed. The only lingering distortion

Moana

A master wayfinder from the island of Motunui, Moana is a strong
and adventurous teenager. Now that she's returned from her voyage
to restore the heart of Te Fiti, Moana enjoys spending time with
her little sister, Simea, and their family. But when she hears a call
from the ancestors to find the lost island of Motufetū, reconnect the
seas, and reunite its people, she can't ignore it—even if that means
leaving her family again.

Kele, a grumpy farmer from the island of Motunui, has always felt a connection to the land. Kele is hesitant to become one of Moana's newest crew members, as he is much more comfortable with his two feet on solid ground. Plus, he doesn't know how to swim! As soon as they set sail, he yearns to return to Motunui and be reunited with his beloved land and crops.

Kele

Loto

Sixteen-year-old Loto is a shipbuilder who loves to learn. An inventor and tinkerer, she constructs top-of-the-line canoes packed with upgrades. Her favorite tool is her adze, which she always carries and wields with abandon—sometimes to the accidental endangerment of others. Moana respects Loto's genius, which is one of the reasons she asks her to join the crew on her next adventure.

Village historian Moni can usually be found in the storytelling fale, recounting wondrous tales to anyone who will listen. His favorite stories to tell? Anything about the demigod Maui, who Moni is totally obsessed with! When he isn't telling stories, Moni can usually be found painting about important current events in real time with incredible speed. Moni knows the ocean's history better than anyone else, making him the perfect addition to Moana's crew as she navigates new waters.

Moni

Matangi

Purple-eyed Matangi is a powerful demigod who has been placed on guard duty inside a giant clam for over one thousand years to prevent anyone from opening the path between realms. Cloaked in mist, Matangi can usually be found moving in the shadows or hanging upside down like a bat with the help of her magical siapo. Peka, her bat companion, will help Matangi carry out her bidding when necessary.

Moana's little sister, Simea, is a spunky and rambunctious three-year-old who absolutely adores her big sis. A curious explorer like Moana, Simea can't wait for her sister to teach her everything she knows about wayfinding. Simea is upset when Moana leaves for her journey to Motufetū. But she finds comfort in the fact that the ocean will connect them while Moana's away. There's no place Simea can go where Moana won't be.

Simea

Heihei

Pua

Pua and Heihei are Moana's animal friends from Motunui. Pua, an adorable pig, can be fearful at times, but he is always willing to follow his pal Moana into dangerous territory. Heihei, a rooster, is quite birdbrained, but he often surprises those around him by accidentally saving the day. Moana is glad to have her animal friends with her on her latest voyage.

Maui

Maui, demigod of the wind and sea and hero to all, is a charismatic and larger-than-life friend of Moana's. With the magical hook he wields (and often loses), he can shape-shift into different animals, from a gigantic whale to a teeny, tiny insect. Big, muscled, athletic, resourceful, and covered in tattoos, Maui will always look out for Moana, even if he doesn't want to admit it at first.

was the feeling that she was still suspended, her body gently swinging back and forth in the air. She saw Loto and Kele doing a strange happy dance on the deck of the canoe, thrilled to be free of the giant clam at last. Loto grabbed Pua and planted a big kiss on his nose. Nearby, Kotu did a celebratory dance with Heihei while Moni tried to come to terms with the fact that he had just been in a portal of the gods.

Everyone was there with her except Maui.

"How'd? What'd? Wait, where's Maui? I gotta find . . ." She struggled, trying to get free of whatever was holding her in a suspended state. Slowly, she spun around . . . to find Maui looking right at her. She had been hanging from his hook by her shoulder strap the whole time.

" 'Sup, Curly," Maui said, giving her one of his trademark grins.

"Maui!" Moana cried happily. She reached to give him a hug but was pulled back by the hook. As soon as Maui dropped her to the ground, she threw her arms around him. She had been too shocked before to fully realize how happy she was to see her friend. Now she couldn't stop smiling. "I did it!" she said, when she finally pulled away.

Maui nodded. His expression was hard to read. "Oh yeah, ya did it," he said.

Ignoring the low-key response, she turned her attention to Mini Maui. "Hey, buddy," she said to the tattoo. "I missed you." She reached up and gave him a high five. Then, realizing she had just high-fived Maui's chest, she stepped back.

"That's weird. Was that weird?" Moana said.

Moni popped up between Moana and Maui. "This is the greatest day of my life!" Moni cheered. He was holding up a new siapo, which showed Moana high-fiving Maui's chest with Moni in between them. "I made more pictures of us!"

Maui raised an eyebrow. "Love this guy . . . Not creeping me out at all," he said. Then he looked at Moana. "Can I talk to you for a second?"

"I can't believe you're here. Where do I start? I was looking for people and couldn't find them, but then the ancestors—Tautai Vasa—he sent a sign, but then the sign exploded and the clam was, like, *CHOMP,* and I was, like, *aaagh. . . .*"

Maui stared at her as she continued to speak quickly. His expression was both happy and annoyed. He was glad to see her, but he really needed to talk to her.

"Anyway, and then Matangi—I mean, whoa, but also *whoa*—but now, like," Moana rambled.

Moana wasn't going to let Maui get a word in. Reaching over, he gently pinched her lips shut.

"Sorry," Moana said around his fingers. "You go."

Maui released her lips. "You're all gonna die."

Moana started to laugh. But one look at Maui's face told her that he wasn't joking. "What?" she asked.

"Nalo didn't just hide Motufetū in a storm," Maui explained. "He hid it in a *monster storm,* from which there is *no escape* . . . and then sank it to the bottom of the sea."

Moana opened her mouth to speak, but Maui kept going.

"Which means A, no human can reach it. And B, ya can't get home unless I beat the storm, which is not a guarantee. Which is why I didn't want you coming in the first place. 'Cause now you're gonna die, your crew's gonna die, and this time so is the chicken. But yeah, it *is* good to see you."

Moana's stomach dropped. Her head spun as she tried to process what Maui had just said.

"What?"

Moana turned at the sound of something behind

her. Her crew was standing there, staring at her. They had heard everything.

Just then, there was a *whoosh* and the canoe, along with the stunned crew, was shot out of the kaleidoscopic tunnel and into the night.

Moana looked at the unfamiliar sea surrounding them. There were no landmarks in sight. Above them, the stars twinkled brightly.

"Good one, Maui. But this place looks perfectly . . . nice," Moana said, trying to laugh off the fear that had filled her since he had told her they were doomed. Moana scanned the sky until she spotted what she was looking for—the constellation above Motufetū! She could see it!

She told the crew that maybe they just needed to sail to it. "Right? Think about it. The ancestors wouldn't

have called if we couldn't do this. . . ." She hoped she sounded more confident than she was feeling.

"Unless it was a butt-dial," Maui said. Then he shook his head. "That'll make sense in two thousand years."

Choosing to ignore whatever that meant, Moana went on, trying to build herself and her crew up. She nodded at Maui. "The fire in the sky took us to *you,*" she pointed out. "Maybe we're supposed to break this curse together. You raise the island, and I step foot on it. And then the curse goes bye-bye." She pretended to be a crowd, cheering them on. Maui bit back a smile. "Maui and Moana together again! Right, Ocean? Ocean . . . ?"

Maui shook his head. "Moana, the ocean cannot help you here," he said.

Frustrated, she looked back to the sky. There had to be a way to finish what they'd started. She just needed a sign.

And then, on the horizon, a familiar blue glow appeared. It was coming straight toward them. Moana's face lit up. Could it be Tautai Vasa?

"Gramma!" she cheered.

Maui followed her gaze. His eyes widened and he began to shake his head. That wasn't Gramma Tala.

That was a massive, hungry, glowing eel!

A moment later, the monster burst out of the water, mouth open, teeth bared. In one quick move, Kotu shot it with blow darts. As the monster sank back beneath the surface, Maui gave the Kakamora an impressed nod. Then, pulling the sail, he nodded to the rest of the crew. He had finally learned their names, but he didn't have the time to call each of them out. "Humans, get to your positions, work together, and let's do this."

They all leapt into action. Only, they didn't know what they were doing and ended up just scrambling around. All the while, more eels were approaching.

Moana bit her lip as Maui turned to her, one eyebrow cocked. "They don't know how to sail?" he asked. "Really gotta talk about your recruiting process."

There was no time to waste. Moana grabbed the oar and began to steer around the glowing eels. "Well, we kinda fell in a clam," she pointed out. If they had been able to keep sailing, she was sure they would all be experts by now.

Maui shook his head. "Gramps, down below!" he ordered. He grabbed Kele and opened the cargo hold. A pile of mudskippers stared up at him. He shuddered.

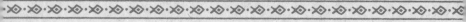

"Hate these guys," he said, before shoving Kele in with them.

"Hey!" Kele protested. "I'm an elder!"

"And I'm three thousand years old! Which makes me elder-ER," Maui retorted. With Kele safely stowed, Maui turned just in time to see another eel leaping from the water. "Just gotta outrun 'em till sunrise!"

Loto perked up. "They're nocturnal?" she asked.

Maui shrugged. "Sure," he said. Then, with a *Chee Hoo!,* he took off.

With Maui on the eel, Moana turned her attention back to the constellation. The eels were between her and where she needed to go. But not for long. "Moni, help me on the oar!" she shouted. "Loto! Sail!" She glanced over to where Kele peeked out from the cargo hold. "Kele, help with Heihei and Pua," she told him.

While the others did what they were told, Moana dodged one underwater eel. But suddenly, another slammed into them from beneath the canoe. The canoe lurched and Moni lost his balance. He fell off the side of the canoe—right into the open mouth of an eel!

Moana screamed.

In one swift move, Maui went in after him. A moment later, there was a flash of explosive light and

Maui reappeared, hauling Moni with him. Dumping him onto the canoe, he shot Moana a look. No more playing. It was time to get out of here.

Moana was exhausted. Fighting their way through the gigantic eels and to the safety of a small atoll had drained her. And from the looks of it, her crew was in no better shape. Even Maui was tired.

The atoll they had washed up on was no more than a fragment of an island formed around a skeleton of one of the eels. A few straggly trees dotted the edge of the land, but otherwise, it was desolate. Moana's canoe lay wrecked upon the shore.

"We'll figure this out," she said, searching for the right words. "We can . . . we can figure this out. The ancestors—"

"Moana."

At her name, Moana turned. Loto was standing beside a pile of what appeared to be wood. She looked shaken. Walking over, Moana looked down at the remnants of a wrecked canoe. Carved on the side was a familiar symbol.

"Tautai Vasa's canoe," Moana whispered.

Maui peered over her shoulder. "Well, it's a bad time to say I told ya so, so . . ."

That was not what Moana needed to hear right now. She had been holding out hope that somehow, Tautai Vasa had survived. That he had at least found people, if not Motufetū. But now she knew the truth. Her thoughts spinning, she went to the edge of the water. She trailed her fingers through the calm ocean, making a shape in the smooth surface. Tears filled her eyes as she lowered her head.

Behind her, she heard Maui approaching. His shadow loomed over her, but he didn't say anything.

"It's like I don't know anything. Every time I think I know what I'm supposed to do, everything changes. Moni almost died! And he wouldn't even be here if I hadn't . . ." She paused for a moment, the words thick in her throat. "If there's a way out, I can't see it. If there's a way home, I can't see it. And I promised everyone. I promised my sister. What if I . . . if I can't." Her body shuddered as she took a deep, shaky breath. Slowly, she turned to look at Maui . . .

. . . who now had a shark head instead of his regular head.

She frowned. "This is serious."

"Is something distracting you? Is it the hair or the

bod?" he deadpanned. "If anyone should be upset, it's me. Since when do you have a sister?"

Before Moana could answer, Maui shapeshifted again. The shark head disappeared, replaced by a pig head. "I can do this all day. And if I do the bug head, you won't sleep for a week."

Plopping down next to her, he nudged her shoulder. "Come on, dish."

"Simea," Moana said. "She's three. You would've met her, if you ever came to visit." She had meant to sound teasing, but the words came out sharp. He *had* been gone for a long time.

"Three years is like a blip to me, princess," he teased.

Moana shot him a look. "Still not a princess."

"Well, a lot of people think you are," Maui said with a shrug. Then his expression softened. "Look, I, uh, get it." He cleared his throat, clearly uncomfortable with sincerity. "No one likes sucking at their job."

"Why are you even here?" Moana replied. Unshed tears threatened to fall. Moana eyed him. A part of her knew he was struggling. Empathy wasn't Maui's strong suit. But he seemed to be trying—for her. And that dulled the pain a little.

Maui paused before responding. "Because . . . because I've been low before, and I couldn't see my path. And someone came along who I underestimated and she lifted me up. Someone I don't want to underestimate herself now." He caught her eye and gave her a small smile. "You will find your path."

She almost smiled. But then remembered. "I haven't done anything right since I left my island," she said.

"Well, every story has a beginning. Every story also has a middle part. Also, a sad section that everyone just wants to be over to get back to the fun stuff," Maui explained. "You're in that sad, sucky part right now, but there *is* a way out. You want get through it? You just gotta . . . *Chee Hoo!* it."

Moana couldn't help herself. She let out a snort. "Wow, you are so bad at this," she said.

Maui pretended to look offended, but then he shook his head. "I'm the best at this. I was a human. Now I'm a demigod. You never know what's next," he retorted. "And maybe breaking the curse is like you said: a one-two punch. I pull it from the sea, but a human has to land on its shores."

"Through a monster storm," added Moana.

As Maui continued to tell her how she might actually be the one who could defeat Nalo, she began to think that maybe her friend was right. She *had* restored Te Fiti's heart. She *had* been strong and embraced her

destiny. She *had* kept it together under pressure and become best friends with a demigod. Maui said he was better for knowing her. That had to count for something. As did all the times she had pushed aside her fears and followed her heart.

This time was no different. Maybe a bit scarier, true. But she was the only one who could write her story. And she wanted to write a great one. One that ended with her finding Motufetū and reconnecting the people of the ocean. With Maui, and her crew, by her side.

She gave Maui a grateful look. Inspiring speeches might not be his favorite, but he was really good at them.

She would follow her destiny.

One way or another.

Danger was on the horizon. But Moana was ready for it. She had Maui in her corner, and she hoped that her crew would be there, too. Despite what they had been through.

Making her way back, she gave them a small smile. They seemed anxious. She didn't blame them.

"Okay, listen," she began. "I know what I've asked of you is a lot . . . that our canoe is in really rough shape. But together, we—"

She stopped as Loto, Kele, and Moni stepped aside. Behind them was the canoe—and it was repaired!

"We found a way to fix it," Loto said proudly. "With a little help from the ancestors."

Looking closer, Moana saw that they had used materials from Tautai Vasa's canoe to repair hers. They had even taken his symbol and placed it on the side.

"I did decorations," Kele added, nodding at other symbols that had been painted on the side of the canoe. "We used the chicken."

At that moment, Heihei walked by, clucking. Sure enough, his head was covered in paint. He looked even more bedraggled than usual.

Maui laughed. "Now I like this guy," he said.

Moana took a deep breath. The time for joking was over. "To find Motufetū, we have to sail right into the heart of the storm," she said. Her eyes flickered out to the ocean. "Maui will raise the island and we'll land on it. It'll be harder than anything we've faced before. Even Maui. If anyone wants to stay here . . ."

No one moved.

Then Moni stepped forward. "I spent my whole life learning the greatest stories of our people. I never thought I'd get to be a part of one. We're in this together, Moana. All the way."

Kotu stepped forward, holding Moana's oar. He held it out to her, his unspoken message clear. He was with her, too. As she took the oar, he gave her the Kakamora warrior salute.

Loto nodded. "Plus if we stay, when night falls, a bunch of giant eels will eat us."

The sun was sinking below the horizon as Moana, Maui, and the crew set out from the atoll toward the constellation. Beneath the canoe, the waters were growing rougher. A nervous energy sparked among them. Well, most of them.

Maui was doing a set of strange-looking exercises, unbothered by the rocking of the waves. "Been a while since I pulled an island from the sea," he said as he squatted. On his chest, Mini Maui gestured to his legs. "I know I have to bend at the knees. I have great posture." When Mini Maui didn't appear to agree, Maui flicked him straight into his armpit.

Moana double-checked that Pua and Heihei were safely tucked in the cargo hold. As she leaned down, Pua nudged her necklace. "We're gonna make it home," she said, her throat constricting at the thought of the promise she had made her sister.

"Moana?"

Turning at the sound of Kele's voice, she was surprised to find him standing in front of her. In his hand he held the last of his potted plants. It had somehow survived their journey so far.

"Kele?" Moana said, confused. "You okay?"

He looked down at the plant. A single tiny fruit had blossomed on it. He held up the pot. "It chose today to fruit. I didn't think it had it in him. But it did."

Moana was touched. She reached out and patted Kele on the shoulder. From out of nowhere, Moni appeared and did the same.

Kele frowned, the emotional moment gone. "Not you," he sniped.

Before Moana could laugh, Maui's voice rang across the canoe. "Curly," he said, his deep voice even deeper in warning.

Straightening up, she noticed a subtle change in the air. She joined Maui at the bow of the canoe. The sky was blue, cloudless. But something was coming. She could feel it.

And then, out of nowhere, a massive storm appeared. It blocked out the constellation and rose like a monster over the horizon.

"It's a storm, just a big one," Moana said, trying to sound optimistic. "We've been through them before. . . ."

Her voice trailed off as she watched the storm grow, forming tentacle-like waterspouts. Inside them, lightning flashed in strange patterns.

"Well, now I kind of miss the lava monster," Maui said from beside her as one of the tentacles slammed down on the water, sending a wave in their direction.

Turning her back on the storm, Moana gestured for the crew to join her. "Everyone together. Maui, clear a path and we'll be right behind."

Maui nodded. Then he glanced over at Loto. "You, smart-stuff, this would be a good time to check the sundial."

Loto looked confused. "Why? What time is it?"

Maui smiled. That was exactly what he wanted to hear. "It's . . ."

"Maui time!" Moni said, jumping in and stealing Maui's thunder.

Maui shot Moni a look, causing the human to gulp. Maybe stepping on a demigod's line wasn't the *best* idea. Luckily, Maui didn't have time to teach him a lesson.

"Let's lift an island and break a curse!" Maui

shouted, racing to the front of the canoe. Just before he reached the end of the deck, he let out a loud *Chee Hoo!* and shifted into a hawk.

With one mighty flap of his giant wings, he took to the sky and was on his way.

CHAPTER 16

It was all hands on deck as waves crashed over the side of the canoe. But they were holding steady. Maui was going to raise the island. They were going to defeat Nalo. And then, Moana told herself as the canoe rocked violently beneath her, they were going home.

All around the canoe, the crew was doing everything they could to keep them moving forward. For one brief moment, Moana felt a little sliver of hope.

Then she looked ahead.

A huge wall of water was bearing down upon them!

It came closer and closer, blocking out the horizon.

Moana raced over and grabbed the oar with Moni. Loto and Kele found something to hold on to. Then they waited, not sure what would happen next. With all their strength, Moana and Moni managed to keep the canoe straight. It went up, up, up the wall of water. For one moment, the canoe hovered precariously at the crest . . . before plummeting back down.

Unfortunately, they weren't out of danger yet. A water tentacle was approaching. Hearing a shout, she looked up to see Maui. He had returned! His hawk eyes were trained on the tentacle, and just before it moved to strike, he shouted to Moni, "Big Man! Dig the oar!"

Moni didn't have to be told twice. With Moana helping him, they veered out of the way of the tentacle. A moment later, Maui sliced the tentacle with his hook, destroying it.

"Maui, keep going!" Moana shouted as more tentacles appeared. Some merged together, forming a whipping, tornado-like tendril. Once again, Moana and Moni guided the canoe out of its path. The tornado had missed them!

"Yeah!" Moni shouted. "Nalo! We're gonna raise that island."

In answer, the storm growled angrily.

But Maui was impressed. Transforming back, he traded fist bumps with Moni. "My guy, you talk that trash," he said, nearly causing Moni to faint. The demigod was his absolute hero. And up until now, he hadn't really seemed to notice him. If it weren't for the danger of Nalo's watery tentacles killing them, he would have immortalized the moment on a siapo.

Now wasn't the time. As they watched, the stormy tentacles that Maui had destroyed appeared to regenerate. If Maui had to keep protecting them, he'd never be able to lift the island. Unless . . .

"Wait! I know how you lift the island," Moana said, realizing what they had to do. She looked at Maui. "The storm doesn't care about you."

Maui looked mildly offended. "I'm Maui," he said. "It cares about me."

She shook her head. That's not what she meant. "Nalo's curse is to separate humans," she explained. "It's *us* it wants to stop. If we distract it, you can reach the center, lift the island."

Maui cocked his head. That was not what he had thought she was going to say. He looked to the sky. Then to the center of the storm. Then back at Moana.

"It'll work," she insisted.

For a moment, the canoe was silent.

"So we are the bait," Moni finally said, "for a monster storm of the gods?"

Moana met Maui's gaze. "You keep coming back to help us, you'll never get the island up. We can do it."

As if on cue, a huge boom of thunder echoed over the waves. Nalo was not happy. But Moana's point was made. The god wasn't happy with *her*.

"Go as fast as you can," Maui said. He walked toward the front of the canoe, then stopped and turned. Moana saw that his face was full of emotion. "The reason I didn't come visit," he said, answering the question she had asked back on the atoll, "was 'cause you made me want to be better. You deserve the whole ocean. . . . I wanted you to have it. Watch yourself out there. I could pull up a million islands, but if you're not there to land on them, what's the point?"

Moana swallowed, her own emotions threatening to spill over. But she pushed them down. "See you out there, Maui," she said. She hoped he knew she meant "Thank you."

He smiled. "See you out there, Moana." Then, turning to the crew, he readied himself. It was go time. "Gonna make one heck of a story," he told them just before powering up and transforming into . . . a small fish?

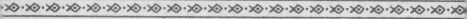

The crew stared at him. That was unexpected.

"So serious," Maui said. He had just been messing with them. "See ya on the island!" With another *Chee Hoo!,* he transformed into a hawk and headed back into the storm.

Dodging lightning, Maui raced toward the storm's center. He hated leaving Moana and her crew behind, but he knew she was right. The humans needed to distract the storm while Maui did his thing. And he knew she would be able to do it. He trusted her.

It didn't take him long to reach the eye of the storm. Inside, it was eerily calm. There were no clouds obscuring the sky. No lightning flashing. And there, hovering over the center of the monstrous storm, was the constellation that had guided Moana and her crew.

Diving down toward the water, Maui shape-shifted from a hawk to a shark. Slicing smoothly through the water, he began to swim. Deeper and deeper he went. His thoughts kept drifting back to Moana, wondering how she was faring up above. The thought of failing her pushed him on as the weight of the water grew heavy.

And then, out of the darkness, a shape appeared.

Vague at first, it became clearer as Maui got closer. Motufetū! He had found it!

Quickly, Maui anchored his hook to the island and attached a rope to the hook. He swam straight to the surface of the water, transformed back into a hawk, and flew with all his might.

Then, with the rope in his talons, he began to pull.

But the island didn't budge. His tattoos glowing, filling his body with the power of the gods, Maui kept going. The rope was taut, the island unmoving. Still he pulled. He strained with everything he had as the tattoos glowed brighter and brighter. . . .

Then the island moved.

Just a bit. But a bit was enough to get the attention of Nalo. The storm let out a thunderous scream and turned toward him.

From the canoe, Moana watched as Maui pulled the rope. She could see how hard the demigod was straining to bring the island up. Maui was doing it! He was actually raising Motufetū!

BOOM!

Out of the storm, a huge blue lightning bolt fired down at Maui. He managed to duck out of the way, but the lightning grazed him. Moana saw him grimace. He continued to pull.

Moana had to do something. She knew Maui wouldn't stop, no matter how many times Nalo sent lightning lashing into him. But a direct hit? Even a demigod couldn't survive that.

Grabbing her conch shell from her belt, she blew into it. The sound caused the storm to turn its attention back on her. It seemed unsure of who to strike next—Maui or Moana. With a roar, it shot a bolt at Moana. It missed. Barely.

"I got it!" Maui shouted over the noise of the storm. "Stay back!"

It went against every instinct, but Moana knew she had to listen to him.

The storm, furious at Maui's progress, let loose the biggest bolt of lightning yet. It slammed into Maui, and it was a direct hit. Electricity wrapped around him, making his body seize horribly. From the canoe, Moana and the crew watched in horror as he tried to fight through it. He still clutched the rope attaching him to the island. But he couldn't possibly hold on much longer.

Then another bolt of lightning ripped into him. Moana let out a cry. Her eyes met Maui's. He gave her a sad, crooked smile. Everything else faded. It was just the two of them, stuck in this moment. And Moana knew, without a word, that Maui was saying goodbye.

"Maui . . . ," she said, her voice small. Tears streamed down her face.

"Find your way, kid," she heard him say over the waves.

And then Maui began to pull again. Using every last ounce of his strength, he lifted the island. It was just at the surface now. Moana could make out the shadows of land below the roiling waves. If he could just get it a bit higher . . .

Nalo wasn't going to let that happen. The lightning wrapped tighter around Maui and sizzled with renewed energy. It racked Maui's body, the power so strong that it peeled the tattoos from his body. Moana gasped. Moni cried out. Loto and Kele keened. This was a punishment that could only be inflicted by the gods. A punishment perhaps worse than anything.

As Mini Maui burned up, Maui finally let out a cry of agony. There was a mighty *boom,* and he was shot into the sky. He seemed to fly up forever, and then there was a pause, his body suspended in the air.

Moana watched, her heart breaking, as he began to fall. "MAUI!" she screamed, her voice raw and aching with emotion.

Her cry was swallowed up by the storm. With Maui

out of the way, the storm barreled toward them, covering them in darkness.

The darkness engulfed Moana. Muffled thunder boomed,
and beneath her, she felt the canoe shifting on water
she couldn't see. The frightened voices of Loto, Moni,
and Kele called out her name, bouncing on the mist.

Losing her footing, Moana stumbled. She gasped as
she felt her necklace pop open and her shell—Simea's
shell—toppled out. Frantically, she searched for it,
ignoring the danger around her. She couldn't lose that
shell. She had already lost so much.

Suddenly, her fingers touched the rough edges of the
shell and she let out a sigh of relief as she closed her
hand around it. When it was safely tucked back in the
necklace, she stood up.

She was going to follow through with her promise.

Standing on the canoe, she thought of Maui. He had
sacrificed so much for her. She thought of her family.
They had put their trust in her. The village believed
in her. Even the ancestors had seen something in her.

She was a wayfinder. She was a tautai. Closing her

eyes, she blocked out the storm. Looking deep into herself, she searched for a solution. Matangi's advice echoed softly in the corners of her mind. *A true way-finder has no idea where they're going. That's the whole point. Finding your way to what's never been found.* In her mind's eye she saw the tunnel, with the dark fork she had been so scared to travel down.

Her eyes popped open. She knew what she had to do!

"Maui doesn't need to raise the island to break the curse. There's another way," she said, her voice growing stronger as the idea took hold. "There's another way! I'll go beyond."

Taking a deep breath, she dove into the swirling darkness.

The crew called out her name, their voices filled with worry. But she couldn't let them stop her. Not now. Not when they were so close.

Immediately, she was enveloped in cool water. Somewhere above her, she could hear the screams of the storm. Nalo's screams. Lightning flashed, illuminating the sky and filtering through the water. Moana hoped that her crew was okay. That Maui had somehow survived.

She kept swimming, her lungs aching, her arms and

legs pushing through the liquid. She just needed to get to the island and touch it.

Another bolt of lightning illuminated the water, revealing Motufetū a few hundred yards below! It was slowly sinking back to the ocean's bottom. The water vibrated around her as Nalo shot another angry bolt of lightning down after her. It missed her, but she knew it was dangerously close.

Doubling down, Moana swam harder. Her lungs screaming for air, she reached the island. She pulled Simea's shell from her necklace and planted it in the soft soil of the island.

For the briefest moment, her fingers brushed against the land.

Then lightning slammed into her.

Her world went black.

Maui found himself back on Moana's canoe. He had survived his encounter with Nalo—barely. After he'd crashed into the ocean, Moni had spotted him. The crew had rescued him and brought him on board.

When he looked at their faces, he knew—Moana had gone after Motufetū herself. His power was nearly drained, his tattoos returning slowly. His hook was missing, but he didn't care.

Maui dove in after Moana.

With what was left of his strength, he swam as fast

as he could. Below him, he could just make out Moana approaching the island.

When the lightning flashed through the water, he could do nothing but watch helplessly as the energy ripped into her body.

When it was over, Moana was still.

Maui let out a strangled cry as he swam toward her. A shock wave blasted off the island, sending him swirling backward. But he pushed through it. Nothing was stopping him from reaching Moana.

Catching her limp body in his arms, he cradled her as his feet sank into Motufetū. He looked down at her. This was not how the story was supposed to end. Spotting Simea's shell, he lowered Moana to lie beside it. Then, kneeling next to her, he put a hand to his heart. It rested on the tattoo of Moana that had appeared after their last adventure. It had been his constant reminder in the three years since how strong a human could be.

As he grieved, the ocean—Moana's ocean!—began to swirl around them, until the ocean created a protective dome over Maui and Moana.

Unaware of anything but Moana, Maui stared down at her, his eyes shimmering with tears. He bowed his head and began to softly chant a prayer to the gods and the ancestors. He didn't know if they could hear him, but he had to try.

To his surprise, he was joined by Tautai Vasa. The huge whale shark glowed, its tattoos bright against the dark waters. And then, as their voices drifted through the waves, more and more spirits appeared. First a few, then dozens. The spirits of the ancestors had answered his calls. They formed a circle around Moana and Maui.

And there, on the ground of Motufetū, Moana gasped.

Maui smiled. Moana was okay.

But she would never be the same.

Moana's eyes fluttered open.

What was going on? The last thing she remembered was reaching out to place Simea's shell on the island. Then there had been a burst of pain, and then . . . nothing.

Sitting up, she saw Maui. And behind him, surrounding them in a huge circle, were the spirits of hundreds of ancestors. She spotted Tautai Vasa. Her eyes scanned farther. There was Gramma Tala!

The ocean shimmered. Moana's oar drifted into her hands. Now it glowed with the patterns of the gods. It was like Maui's hook, but different.

The importance of the ocean's gift flooded Moana. This was a bridge between the people and the ocean, between past and future.

Moana gripped her oar. Then a smile began to tug at her lips.

Turning, she met Maui's gaze. He was staring at her in shocked awe. On his chest, Mini Maui was crying happily. She didn't need either of them to tell her what had happened—she knew that Maui was the reason she was still here. And now he would be by her side when they finished what they had started.

Arching an eyebrow, she nodded over her shoulder. It was time they raised an island—together.

Maui didn't hesitate. He shot to the surface, transforming into a hawk as he hit the air. The sun was shining down on the water, and the blue skies were cloudless. Once again, he grasped the rope in his talons and pulled.

Below him, the water started to roil as Motufetū began to rise. With a huge splash, the island burst past the surface of the ocean. On top of it stood Moana.

She looked out and saw the whole ocean before

her. She spotted her canoe and the crew, their mouths hanging open, safely floating in the calm water. She saw Maui, hovering nearby, a familiar comfort in this uncharted territory.

Taking a deep breath, she lifted her conch shell to her lips and blew into it. The sound exploded across the waves. As it reached the water, the ocean channels that had been dormant since Motufetū sank opened. Now the people, once kept away by Nalo's curse, would be reunited.

The sound of flapping wings alerted her to the arrival of Maui. He landed next to her, transforming from hawk to demigod. He gave her a smile, his eyes filled with pride.

Hearing a commotion on the shore, she looked down to see the canoe, with her eager crew aboard, arriving. Before the canoe had even stopped fully, they raced toward her. She took off at a run, too, launching herself at them in the biggest, best group hug of her life. She hadn't realized, until that very moment, how much they all meant to her. Maui had saved her, but they had, too.

"Can I just—? Let me get into the—" Maui landed next to the group and began to try to wiggle into the hug. But no one was letting go anytime soon. Finally, he shifted into a lizard, popped himself inside the group, then transformed back into a demigod.

The moment was interrupted when a huge wave splashed over them.

Pulling herself free, Moana looked over and saw the ocean forming a familiar wave. "Ocean!" she said happily. "I missed you!"

Maui shrugged. "I'm fifty-fifty," he said, earning himself a spray of water directly in his face.

As the others laughed, Moana took a moment to look at the gathered group. They had believed in her, and together they had raised Motufetū.

They had opened the seas.

The sun was sinking toward the horizon as Moana, Maui, and the rest of the crew stood in front of a rocky wall on Motufetū. The surface was weather-worn, algae and coral still clinging to its side from its time submerged in the water. But clearly etched into the side was an image of Motufetū. The island's symbol was depicted as the head of an octopus, its eight long tentacles representing the channels of the sea.

"Now that the channels are open, you think people will come back?" Moni asked.

Moana had been contemplating that same question.

And while she wasn't sure, she had thought of another option. "Or maybe we'll go to them. . . ."

The thought settled over the crew. For a moment they were silent, all lost in the significance of what that might mean.

The moment was broken by Maui. Crouched beside Pua, he was staring at the pig. "Raisin' an island really works up an appetite," he said. "Know what I'm saying?"

Moana swooped in and picked up Pua. She gave Maui a scolding look and was about to tell him— again—that Pua was a friend, not food, when the unmistakable blare of a conch shell wailed in the distance!

She froze as all eyes turned to her. She hadn't made that sound. Glancing at Heihei to make sure the trouble-some rooster hadn't found her conch, she saw that he was pecking Maui on the nose, oblivious. So if it wasn't Heihei, and it wasn't her . . .

The sound came again. Racing over, she peeked through a hole in the wall. She scanned the horizon and then gasped. There, faint but growing clearer, was the unmistakable silhouette of a canoe.

"People?" she cried. "It's PEOPLE!"

With her crew behind her, Moana ran to the shore.

She skidded to a stop on the sandy beach just as a canoe landed. There was a moment when both crews simply stared, stunned by each other's presence. Then the wayfinder of the new crew leapt off the canoe and sprinted excitedly toward Moana.

As Moana and the new wayfinder met, another conch echoed over the ocean. And then another! People were arriving from all over! It was more than Moana could have ever hoped for.

They were here. The people were here! And they would never be separated again.

As joyful cheers filled the air, Moana smiled broadly. They had raised Motufetū. Just like she had promised. But now there was one more part of that promise she had to keep. . . .

The shores of Motunui were peaceful, sparkling in the sun. In the village, people went about their days, unaware of what had transpired oceans away.

Suddenly, there was an explosion of sand. When it cleared, Maui stood there. Brushing himself off, he glanced around. The villagers on the beach froze in awe at his sudden appearance.

"And he sticks the landing!" he said proudly.

Shaking off the shock, several young boys slid out of a nearby coconut tree and stared slack-jawed at Maui. They had heard stories of the demigod, but now he was here! On Motunui! Others came closer, eyes wide. Maui soaked up the attention.

"Yup, breathe it in. Sorry about the mess," he said. Then he remembered why he was there. "Looking for a Simea? Mini Moana? Is there a—"

"*I'm* Simea," a small voice said. Maui looked down. Staring up at him, with big eyes that looked very familiar, was a little girl. She was covered in sand from his landing. He leaned down to brush some off, but to his surprise, she grabbed his ear and added, "Of Motunui."

Maui nodded. This also felt familiar. "Ha, yeah, you're her," he confirmed. He gestured for her to let go of his ear. When she finally did, he straightened and went on. "Your sister sent me, actually, with a present for ya."

At the mention of Moana, Simea's eyes lit up. She clapped and danced on her toes, eager for the present.

Maui searched through his grass skirt for something. "Here ya go," he said, holding out a circular seashell. "Straight from Motufetū."

Simea took it and turned it over in her hand, confused. "What's it do?"

Maui leaned over and lifted the shell. There was a hole in the center. He gestured for her to peer through it.

Slowly, she held it up to her eye. And then she gasped. There, bursting over the reef, was Moana! She stood at the front of the canoe, her crew behind her. She had come home!

"*Little sis!*" Moana cried out, her voice carrying over the waves.

"*BIG SIS!*" Simea shouted back, racing into the shallow water.

Moana leapt from the canoe, the ocean parting for her so she could run to Simea. They crashed into each other a moment later, laughing and crying at the same time. And then their mom and dad were there as well, throwing their arms around Moana.

When they finally pulled apart and made it back to the beach, Chief Tui smiled down at his daughter. "So," he asked, "how'd it go this time?"

They all turned to watch as dozens of canoes from all over the ocean appeared on the horizon. Meeting her father's gaze, Moana smiled.

Moana and her crew had spent the first few days after their arrival at Motunui settling back into their old routines and welcoming the new visitors who had landed on their shores. Loto and another engineer came up with a plan to build a super-canoe, Kele shared some new fruit with his apprentice, and Moni told the story of their adventure to an eager crowd.

Life went back to normal, but nothing was the same. The whole crew, not just Moana, had changed on their voyage. And the arrival of new people to Motunui had opened up new worlds.

But after things began to settle down, Moana knew there was one thing left to do. So with Kotu aboard, she and Maui had sailed back to Kakamora Island and returned him to his family. The very last of her promises, kept.

Now Moana and Maui stood at the front of her canoe. Behind them, the home island of the Kakamora faded into the distance.

"Where to?" Maui asked his dear friend.

Moana wasn't sure what the future held, but she was ready to find out. Raising the sail, she turned to Maui. "Might want to hold on," she said, smiling.

EPILOGUE

Night had fallen in a distant realm, far from Motufetū. But for some of those residing in the darkness, the impact of what Moana and Maui had done felt all too close.

Arriving in a flurry of bats, Matangi, newly freed from her clam prison, glided to the ground. The thick fog around her instantly vanished as . . . *BOOM!* Lightning exploded at her feet, stopping her in her tracks.

She glanced down, her purple eyes narrowing. The lightning had ignited a small flame. She casually stepped on the flame to extinguish it. Well, that hadn't been a very pleasant greeting. But she wasn't surprised. She knew exactly who had flung the bolts.

"You missed, Nalo," she hissed, not even attempting to keep the annoyance from her voice.

A moment later, a figure emerged from the thinning fog. Sculpted from storm clouds, the figure was immense, with two glowing white eyes that bored into Matangi. They looked like lightning. While his head and torso were human-like, the figure had smoke for legs. He let out a grumble that echoed through the space.

It was Nalo.

Nalo sent another bolt of lightning—only this time, he zapped Peka. Peka flew off, smoldering. Matangi rolled her eyes, unimpressed. Nalo didn't frighten her. In fact, right now, he just made her mad.

"A human should never have been able to reach Motufetū," he said in a voice that sounded like the rumbling of thunder. "Or break my curse."

Matangi paused, carefully considering her words. Moana had surprised her. She wasn't the weak, whiny human she had expected. Moana had more passion, strength, courage, and conviction than most of the gods and demigods Matangi knew. She would never say it out loud, of course, but she had been proud of

Moana. . . . The girl had figured her way out. Plus Moana had set Matangi free in the process. "Well, I'm not sure . . . ," she said after a beat, "she's what you thought she was."

That was not the answer Nalo wanted. Now he was seething. He started to rise.

"Then her story must end!"